Landmarks of world literature

Laurence Sterne

TRISTRAM SHANDY

Landmarks of world literature

General Editor: J. P. Stern

LAURENCE STERNE

Tristram Shandy

WOLFGANG ISER

Translated by David Henry Wilson

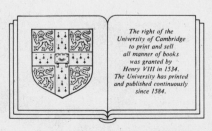

The right of the
University of Cambridge
to print and sell
all manner of books
was granted by
Henry VIII in 1534.
The University has printed
and published continuously
since 1584.

CAMBRIDGE UNIVERSITY PRESS
Cambridge
New York   New Rochelle   Melbourne   Sydney

Published by the Press Syndicate of the University of Cambridge
The Pitt Building, Trumpington Street, Cambridge CB2 1RP
32 East 57th Street, New York, NY 10022, USA
10 Stamford Road, Oakleigh, Melbourne 3166, Australia

First published 1988

Printed in Great Britain at
the University Press, Cambridge

British Library cataloguing in publication data
Iser, Wolfgang
Laurence Sterne: Tristram Shandy. –
(Landmarks of world literature).
1. Sterne, Laurence, *1713–1768*. Tristram
Shandy
I. Title   II. Series
823′.6   PR3714

Library of Congress cataloguing in publication data
Iser, Wolfgang.
Laurence Sterne: Tristram Shandy / Wolfgang Iser: translated by
David Henry Wilson.
p.   cm. – (Landmarks of world literature)
Bibliography: p.
ISBN 0-521-32807-1. ISBN 0-521-31263-9 (pbk.)
1. Sterne, Laurence, 1713–1768. Life and opinions of Tristram
Shandy, gentleman. I. Title. II. Series.
PR3714. T73184   1988
823′.6 – dc 19   87-31164
CIP

ISBN 0 521 32807 1 hard covers
ISBN 0 521 31263 9 paperback

Contents

Preface

My sincere thanks are due to The Institute for Advanced Studies at the Hebrew University, Jerusalem, who granted me a Fellowship that enabled me to write this book. I am most grateful for the hospitality and support given to me by all the staff and for the magnificent organisation provided by Sanford Budick. I benefited greatly from talks with other fellows, and in particular from my discussions with Stanley Cavell.

My thanks also to Cambridge University Press, and in particular to Professor Peter Stern, who first approached me with the idea for the book, and to Terence Moore, who welcomed it despite its maverick nature.

Finally, once again I am deeply indebted to David Henry Wilson for rendering my German into readable English.

For the sake of easy access, I have quoted from readily obtainable editions of Sterne and Locke: all *Tristram Shandy* references are to the Signet Classic edition, New York 1980, with an afterword by Gerald Weales, (quoted by book, chapter, page), while those to Locke's *Essay concerning Human Understanding* are based on John W. Yalton's edition, Everyman's Library, London 1971, (quoted by book, chapter, paragraph).

Chronology*

	Sterne's life and works	Related literary and historical events
1711		J. Addison and R. Steele edit *Spectator*; David Hume born;
1712		Handel goes to London; final witch trials in London;
1713	Laurence Sterne born November 24 at Clonmel, Tipperary, Ireland, where his father, ensign Roger Sterne, was stationed; long journeys and migrations during the subsequent ten years;	Treaty of Utrecht with the famous Asiento; Denis Diderot born; Shaftesbury dies;
1714		Tory ministry collapses after the death of Queen Anne; George I succeeds to the throne; personal union between England and Hanover; Handel, *Water Music*;
1715	family moves to Dublin;	Louis XIV, *Roi du Soleil* dies; first excavations of Pompeii and Herculaneum;
1716		first American theatre in Williamsburg; G.W. Leibniz dies;
1717		Maria Theresia born; Freemasonry in London; vaccination against smallpox in England;
1718	on the move again – from Bristol to Hampshire to Dublin again;	Declaration of war against Spain; Halley discovers movement of the fixed stars;
1719		Daniel Defoe, *Robinson Crusoe*; Handel becomes director of the London opera;

1720	six months with Mr Fetherston and his family near Wicklow; the miraculous escape, falling into a mill-race while the mill was in operation, and being rescued unhurt;	*Robinson Crusoe* translated into German; opening of Old Haymarket Theatre in London; Canaletto born;
1721	Chudleigh's regiment moves again to Dublin;	Robert Walpole, leader of Whigs, first English Prime Minister till 1742; Watteau dies; J.S. Bach, *Brandenburg Concertos*;
1722	in Dublin barracks Laurence learns to read and write; taken to England, separated from his family;	John Churchill, Duke of Marlborough, dies;
1723	enrolled at school, Hipperholme, with Nathan Sharpe as his master and friend;	Joshua Reynolds born; Adam Smith born;
1724	learns to read and write Latin and Greek and acquires a good knowledge of classical literature;	F.G. Klopstock born; Immanuel Kant born; Paris Stock Exchange opens;
1725	Jacques Sterne receives Doctor of Law from Jesus College, Cambridge;	Peter I (the Great) dies; Pope translates *Odyssey* into English; Casanova born;
1726		Swift, *Gulliver's Travels*; after being arrested at the Bastille twice, Voltaire goes to England;
1727	Roger Sterne's regiment ordered to Gibraltar, where he is severely wounded in a dual with a fellow officer;	George I dies, George II succeeds to the throne; Pope, Swift and Arbuthnot publish *Miscellanies*; Thomas Gainsborough born; Newton dies; American Philosophical Society founded in Philadelphia;
1728		John Gay, *The Beggar's Opera*;
1729		Catharine II (the Great) born; G.E. Lessing born;
1730	Roger's regiment sent from Gibraltar to Jamaica to fight a slave uprising;	James Thomson, *The Seasons*;

	Sterne's life and works	Related literary and historical events
1731	Roger dies of fever at Port Antonio; his mother tries to settle in England, but has to return to Ireland; Laurence remains with Mr Sharpe another year;	Daniel Defoe dies;
1732	Richard Sterne dies; Laurence left without any friends;	George Washington born (first President of the USA); Voltaire, *Zaïre*; Joseph Haydn born; Academy of Ancient Music in London; Pope, *Essay on Man*;
1733	spends a year with young Richard Sterne at Elvington; on July 6, Sterne registers *in absentia* at Jesus College, Cambridge; arrives five days later;	
1734	receives one of the scholarships that Archbishop Sterne had designated for poor boys of Yorkshire or Nottinghamshire;	Franz Mesmer born;
1735	makes friends, matriculates and prepares for his examinations;	
1736	friendship with John Hall-Stevenson and John Fountayne begins;	James Watt born;
1737	B.A. at Jesus College; assistant curate of St Ives;	Antonio Stradivari dies;
1738	admitted to priesthood by Samuel Peploe, Bishop of Chester, at a special ordination held in the cathedral church of Chester; vicar at Sutton-upon-Forest, near York;	John Wesley, his brother Charles, and George Whitefield establish Methodist movement;
1739	hires Richard Wilkinson as his assistant curate, a rather unusual move;	Hume, *Treatise of Human Nature*;
1740	the names of Peter Torriano, Frederick Keller and Laurence Sterne appear together in the *Grace Book* of Cambridge, presumably after they had become Masters of Arts;	Karl VI, German emperor, dies, Karl VII succeeds to the throne; Frederick William I of Prussia dies; Frederick II (the Great) succeeds to the throne; Samuel Richardson, *Pamela*; University of Philadelphia founded;

1741	marries Elizabeth Lumley; becomes prebendary in York Minster; chief writer for the Whigs in the by-election;	David Garrick, Sterne's friend, plays Richard III in London;
1742	enters politics on the side of a temporary organisation of Walpole supporters; open and bitter quarrel between Jacques and Laurence Sterne, uncle and nephew, reaching its climax in the years 1747–51; *The York Gazeteer, Query upon Query*;	Fielding, *Joseph Andrews*; Edward Young, *Night Thoughts*; Edmund Halley dies;
1743	goes to Stillington, adjoining Sutton; publishes 'The unknown world, verses occasioned by hearing a pass-bell' in *The Gentleman's Magazine*;	Thomas Jefferson born (second President of the USA); Antonio Vivaldi dies;
1744	Sterne's cousin Richard dies; on November 1 purchases the Tindal Farm at Sutton;	Frederick II starts Second Silesian War; Jean Paul Marat born; Alexander Pope dies;
1745	till 1759 immense reading activity; a daughter named Lydia born and baptised on October 1 and buried the next day;	Prince Charles Edward Stuart returns to Britain; Jonathan Swift dies;
1746		
1747	'The case of Elijah and the widow of Zarephath, consider'd' preached at St Michael le Belfry; published the same year; probably composed most of his sermons during the decade after he settled in Sutton 1742–51; with John Fountayne drawn into chapter affairs; on December 1 a daughter is born;	war in South-India between England and France;
1748		Treaty of Aix-la-Chapelle; Samuel Richardson, *Clarissa*; Jeremy Bentham born; David Hume, *Enquiry Concerning Human Understanding*; Voltaire, *Zadig*;

	Sterne's life and works	Related literary and historical events
1749		Henry Fielding, *Tom Jones*; Johann Wolfgang von Goethe born; Johann Sebastian Bach dies;
1750	attends seven of eleven chapter meetings to help Fountayne, and because he is personally concerned with the question of substitutes; sworn in as Lord Fauconberg's commissary; Dean Fountayne seeks to reconcile the estranged mother, son, and uncle;	
1751	antiquarian studies, anthropological studies; Elizabeth delivered of a dead child; sworn in as the dean's substitute;	Tobias Smollett, *The Adventures of Peregrine Pickle*; the first volumes of the *French Encyclopaedia* published (35 vols. by 1780); the Blue Stockings meet in London;
1752	exchanges letters with Blake about his farming, the weather and parish business;	
1753	Justice of the Liberty; out of favour with Archbishop of York, so that his former curate, Richard Wilkinson, is preferred when the perpetual curacy of Coxwold becomes vacant; recommends Hogarth's *The Analysis of Beauty* to his readers; preferred authors are Lucian, Rabelais, Cervantes, Robert Burton (*The Anatomy of Melancholy*) and John Locke (*Essay on Human Understanding*);	George Berkeley dies; Hogarth, *The Analysis of Beauty*;
1754		George Washington clashes with French troops near Fort Duquesne;
1755	the private and political war with his uncle comes to an end;	colonial war between England and France (till 1763); earthquake destroys Lisbon; Frederick II captures Dresden; Seven Years' War; Wolfgang Amadeus Mozart born;
1756	professional and business affairs are finally on a relatively sound footing;	

1757	Newcastle and William Pitt, the elder, settle on a coalition cabinet, with Newcastle in charge of domestic and Pitt of foreign affairs; riots over the high cost of food; Horatio Nelson born; Samuel Johnson, *Rasselas*;
1758	involved in local scandal; Elizabeth's psychological condition badly affected; lively correspondence between Sterne and John Blake, Master of the Royal Grammar School; Sterne's daughter Lydia in bad health;
1759	moves with his family to York; publishes *A Political Romance* (History of a good warm watch-coat); publishes Vols. I and II of *Tristram Shandy* in York (London edition, January 1, 1760); reluctantly heeds advice of his clerical friends that the *Romance* be suppressed; burns the copies (but not all!);	William Pitt, the younger, born; Robert Burns born; Friedrich von Schiller born; Voltaire, *Candide*;
1760	lionised in London, presented with the living at Coxwold; Shandy Hall; Dodsley announces a new edition of *Tristram Shandy*; Sterne promises a fresh volume every year; publishes *The Sermons of Mr Yorick*, May and June 1760;	the Russians in Berlin; George II dies, George III succeeds to the throne;
1761	publishes Vols. III and IV of *Tristram Shandy*, June 1760–May 1761; Vols. V and VI of *Tristram Shandy* in London, June 1761–January 1762; meets Dr Johnson;	Jean-Jacques Rousseau, *La Nouvelle Héloïse*;

Sterne's life and works

1762 January–June, travels in France although the dreaded disease of his youth (consumption) has broken out again; arrives in Paris on January 16 or 17, completely exhausted by the journey, yet recovers very rapidly to the surprise of his physicians; stays in France from August 1762 till May 1764;

1763 installs himself with his family in Toulouse;

1764 wants to return to Coxwold; leaves his wife and daughter in the South of France; stops on his way back in Paris, where he meets old friends; this season Hume is the great sensation of Paris society;

1765 Yorkshire and London: *Tristram Shandy*, Vols. VII and VIII, June 1764–April 1765;

1766 publishes Vols. III and IV of *The Sermons of Mr Yorick*; a tour of Italy from October 1765 till May 1766; witnesses a fresh eruption of Vesuvius; sits for a portrait bust in terracotta by Nollekens;

1767 the last Vol. (IX) of *Tristram Shandy*, June 1766–March 1767; at Coxwold his health declines rapidly; Ignatius Sancho, a former slave, writes famous letter asking Sterne to handle the subject of slavery in his next book and thus draw public attention to it (cf. *TS* IX/6); prepares publication

Related literary and historical events

1762 Catherine II, Tsarina of Russia; Jean-Jacques Rousseau, *Emile*; Johann Gottlieb Fichte born; Jean-Jacques Rousseau, *Du Contrat Social*;

Peace of Paris; Jean Paul born; Mozart on concert tour through Europe;

1764 Horace Walpole, *The Castle of Otranto*; William Hogarth dies; Jean Philippe Rameau dies;

1766 Lessing, *Laokoon oder über die Grenzen der Malerei und Poesie*;

1767 August Wilhelm Schlegel born; Wilhelm von Humboldt born; Georg Philipp Telemann dies;

of the *Sermons of Mr Yorick* and has a vision of
1,000 guineas before a word of the book is written;
The Journal to Eliza, March–October 1767;
friendship with Mrs Draper from January 1767 till
April 1767, when she leaves for India to meet her
husband;

1768   *A Sentimental Journey*, June 1767–February 1768;
a hard winter brings influenza, which leads to
pleurisy; Laurence Sterne dies at 4 p.m. on Friday,
March 18.

1769   *Sermons by the Late Reverend Mr Sterne* (3 vols.).

François René Chateaubriand born; Friedrich
Schleiermacher born.

Further history of *Tristram Shandy*

1759–67   Vols. I–II first edn York, 1759; (2nd edn London: Dodsley, 1760)
            Vols. III–IV London: Dodsley, 1761
            Vols. V–VI London: Becket and Dehondt, 1762
            Vols. VII–VIII London: Becket and Dehondt, 1765
            Vol. IX London: Becket and Dehondt, 1767

1765   *Das Leben und die Meynungen des Herrn Tristram Shandy*, transl. by J.F. Zückert, Berlin und
            Stralsund (6 vols.)

1774   *Tristram Shandis Leben und Meynungen*, transl. by J. Bode, 9 parts, Hamburg (2nd rev. edn, 1776)

1776–85   *La Vie et les Opinions de Tristram Shandy*, transl. by M. Frénais, York et Paris: Ruoult (2 vols.)

1779   *Het Leven en de Gevoelens van Tristram Shandy*, transl. by Bernardus Brunius, Amsterdam:
            Mummithuisen (5 vols.)

1797   *Oeuvres de Laurence Sterne*, transl. by Frénais and D.L.B. (de la Beaume), Paris (6 vols.)

1804–7   *The Life and Opinions of Tristram Shandy, gentleman*, transl. into Russian by M.S. Kajzarov, St Petersburg (6 vols.)

1816   *The Life and Opinions of Tristram Shandy, gentleman*, with a life of the author, written by himself, New York: Huntington (4 vols.)

1832   *The Life and Opinions of Tristram Shandy, gentleman*, with a life of the author, by Sir Walter Scott, Paris: Baudry

1835   *La vie et les opinions de Tristram Shandy par Sterne*, Paris: A. Hiard

1848   *The Life and Opinions of Tristram Shandy, gentleman*, comprising the humorous adventures of Uncle Toby and Corporal Trim . . . beautifully illustrated by Darley, Philadelphia: Grigg, Elliot & Co.

1848   *The Life and Opinions of Tristram Shandy*, a complete edition, Aberdeen: Clark & Son

1858   *Vie et opinions de Tristram Shandy, gentilhomme* followed by *Voyage sentimental* and *Lettres d'Yorick à Eliza*, par Sterne, transl. by M. Léon de Wailly, Paris: Charpentier

1865   *Tristram Shandy's Leben und Meinungen*, transl. by F.A. Gelbcke, Berlin (2 parts)

1884–5   *Sterne. La vie et les opinions de Tristram Shandy*, 1st and 2nd parts transl. by M. Frénais and 3rd and 4th parts by M. de la Beaume, Paris: Librairie de La Bibliothèque Nationale (4 vols.)

1884   *The Life and Opinions of Tristram Shandy, gentleman*, by Laurence Sterne; with an introduction by Henry Morley. London and New York: Routledge & Sons

1890   *Oeuvres de Laurence Sterne. Vie et opinions de Tristram Shandy*, new translation by A. Hédouin, Paris (4 vols.)

1899   *The Life and Opinions of Tristram Shandy, gentleman*, with an introduction by Wilbur L. Cross, New York and London

1905   *The Life and Opinions of Tristram Shandy, gentleman*, and *A Sentimental Journey through France and Italy*, London: Newnes

1922   *La Vita e le Opinioni di Tristano Shandy*, ed. by Ada Salvatore, Modena: Peraguti

1928   *The Life and Opinions of Tristram Shandy*, with illustrations and decorations by John Austen and an introduction by J.B. Priestley, London and New York

1937   *Das Leben und die Ansichten 'Tristram Shandy'*, transl. into German by Rudolf Kassner, Berlin: Deutsche Buchgemeinschaft

1939   *Leben und Meinungen des Herrn Tristram Shandy*, rev. German edn by Bruno Wolfgang, Berlin

1940   *The Life and Opinions of Tristram Shandy, gentleman*, ed. by James Aiken Work, New York: Odyssey Press

1946   Laurence Sterne, *Vie et opinions de Tristram Shandy, gentilhomme*, transl. by Charles Mouran, Paris: Laffont (1st edn)

1955   *Tristram Shandy, gentleman*, transl. into Serbo-Croatian by S. Vinaver, Belgrade

1958   *Tristram Shandy, gentleman*, transl. into Polish by K. Tarnowska, Warsaw

1963   *Tristram Shandy, gentleman*, transl. into Czech by A. Skoumal, Prague

1965   *The Life and Opinions of Tristram Shandy, gentleman*, ed. by Ian Watt, Boston: Houghton Mifflin Comp.

1967   *The Life and Opinions of Tristram Shandy, gentleman*, ed. by Graham Petrie, introduction by Christopher Ricks, Baltimore: The Penguin English Library

1968   *The Life and Opinions of Tristram Shandy, gentleman*, transl. into Russian and with an introduction by A. Elisatratova, Moscow

1969   *The Life and Opinions of Tristram Shandy, gentleman*, transl. into Romanian and with an introduction by Mihai Miroiu and Mihai Spariosu, Bucharest

1970   *The Life and Opinions of Tristram Shandy, gentleman*, ed. by Graham Petrie, introduction by Gilbert Phelps, London: Folio Society

1972   *Leben und Meinungen von Tristram Shandy, gentleman*, transl. by Otto Weith, Epilogue by Erwin Wolff, Stuttgart

1975   *Tristram Shandy, gentleman*, transl. into Slovak by J. Vojtek, Bratislava

* The chronology, the further history and the bibliography were compiled by Dr Monika Reif-Hülser

Chapter I

Subjectivity revealed through textual fields of reference

1 Does *Tristram Shandy* have a beginning?

The question itself implies that the time-honoured concept of a story as having a beginning, a middle and an end cannot be regarded as the fixed criterion of narration, for *Tristram Shandy* has become a landmark of narrative literature despite its flagrant breach of this convention. Generally the violation of such norms serves to bring out whatever has been concealed by customary expectations. If a story is supposed to have a beginning, a middle and an end, it is for the purpose of exemplifying the point it intends to make. A story that has difficulty with its own beginnings need not be any the less exemplary, but the clear implication is that its exemplarity will be of a different nature: instead of serving to elucidate a specific social, moral or political purpose, for instance, the story may now concern itself with uncovering the presuppositions underlying a beginning.

For the most part novelists of the early eighteenth century paid little attention to such problems. They tended to latch straight on to the traditional formula, either beginning their story *ab ovo* or immediately going *in medias res*, and one can even find variations of the fairy-tale 'once upon a time', as for example at the start of Fielding's *Tom Jones*: 'In that part of the western division of this kingdom which is commonly called Somersetshire, there lately lived, and perhaps lives still, a gentleman whose name was Allworthy' (Henry Fielding, *The History of Tom Jones* I, p. 3).

The advantage of such a conventional starting-point was that it required no explanation, and indeed a drawn-out consideration of how to begin might have detracted from the aim of telling the exemplary story of the hero. In order to perform their deeds, the heroes first had to come into the world, and so their birth was something that could be taken for granted.

In *Tristram Shandy*, however, nothing can be taken for granted. The narrator does not in any way regard his birth as a beginning; indeed it seems to him almost like a doom-laden end: '"*My Tristram's misfortunes*", says Uncle Toby, "*began nine months before ever he came into the world*"' (I, 3, 11), and the italics place full emphasis upon this announcement.

The beginning, then, is already a result, for the birth was preceded by the conception, and this, according to Tristram, raises the question of whether his father and mother

duly considered how much depended upon what they were then doing; – that not only the production of a rational Being was concerned in it, but that possibly the happy formation and temperature of his body, perhaps his genius and the very cast of his mind; – and, for aught they knew to the contrary, even the fortunes of his whole house might take their turn from the humours and dispositions which were then uppermost.   (I, 1, 9)

But what, at this decisive moment, actually preoccupied the father and mother was their own particular association of ideas. Marital duties were normally preceded by the winding of the clock, and at the crucial moment Mother Shandy counters him with a 'silly question'.

If, as Paul Valéry suggests, the novel's point of departure contains its poetics in a nutshell (cf. Norbert Miller, 'Die Rollen des Erzählers', p. 40), what does such a beginning reveal? The answer must be: multilayered problematisation of how to start.

First, the inception may be read as a parody, which would point to a historical reference. For the hero of the eighteenth-century novel, birth is a beginning without question; what matters is his *history*, frequently stressed in the actual titles of the narratives. *History* had specific connotations: it illustrated the testing of norms and ideals by subjecting them to the vicissitudes of time, and even if the Christian origins of such tests tended to fade into the background, this was the pattern that underlay the biographical form of the novel, as Lukács has called it (see *Die Theorie des Romans*, pp. 68–82). It is not by chance that very early on Tristram alludes to Bunyan's *Pilgrim's Progress* (I, 4, 12), for although he has no desire to compete with it, he would like an equally wide reading public for his own narrative. While the path followed so tentatively by Bunyan's pilgrim leads towards the hoped-for certitude of salvation, *history* focuses on the empirical world in order to validate the norms represented by the hero. If *history* is meant to ratify these values, it is still subservient to an overriding purpose, which, in turn, finds its endorsement only through the successful mastery of life's conflicts.

Through this fusion of overall purposes with the reality of experience, the eighteenth-century hero became a carrier of meaning, and his birth – if it was mentioned at all – was no more than the natural beginning of what was to be accomplished by the end. Tristram is no such messenger, and so he does not write a *history* but a *Life*, with no aspirations towards self-perfection, but simply in the sense defined by Dr Johnson's *Dictionary* as a 'Narrative of a Life past'. This kind of *Life* is in direct contrast to the *history*, for instead of binding all events together in an ultimate meaning, it expands each single incident out into its prehistory, showing that the character of events is such that they need not necessarily have taken the course that they did. While the *history* is drawn together by the meaning of its end, the *Life* explodes into the imponderable. The connections between natural and historical processes thus undergo a remarkable inversion: in the *history* type of novel, the hero's birth is the natural precondition for the unfolding of his story; for Tristram, the birth stands at the end of an infinitely expanding range of prehistories. Underlying the *history* is a teleological ordering of its purpose, whereas Tristram's pre-birth life stories are all marked by the workings of chance.

If, however, Tristram's *Life* were written only as a counter to the success story contained in the *history*, then the latent parody would now have nothing but historical interest. But a parody that can outlast the context of its genesis must be more than a mere inversion of an inherited schema.

Since the beginning itself turns out to be a result, with Tristram's misfortunes starting nine months before his birth, it may be said that for the most part the hero can hardly be held responsible for what happens to him. Consequently he is no longer a suitable carrier of meaning in the service of an overall purpose, and so in comparison to his fellow eighteenth-century heroes, Tristram is without a function. Instead of demonstrating something, he himself becomes the object of scrutiny, thus causing a shift in the narrative tradition by opening up hitherto unexplored realms: the hero, having lost his various traditional functions, is now set free to become a subject in his own right; and being thrown back upon himself, as it were, he begins to discover himself in all his difficult complexity.

In the circumstances, it is only logical that the very first sentence of Sterne's novel should allude to the humours as the natural explanation of man's nature. If the hero becomes a self to be focused on, then recourse to his physiological basis is the least determinate approach to defining what the self might be. Whatever it is, it certainly has a body made up of humours. Furthermore, the theory of the humours was one with which eighteenth-century readers were quite familiar, so that whatever may have been its evaluation in *Tristram Shandy*, it was a way of making the new subject-matter of the self accessible to the contemporary public.

Straightaway, however, the double function of this concept finds itself in trouble. The first sentence of the novel reels off a hypotactic string of conditions to be considered when the humours are being constituted, and the following chapter (I, 2, 10f.) then proceeds to discuss the engendering of the homunculus, who may be subject to a thousand weaknesses if the mixture of his fluids should be wrong. Just as the formula for an artificial being remains inaccessible to the philosophers, so too do Tristram's parents remain unaware of what they are starting.

By showing how inexplicable are the forces that govern the physiological interplay of the humours, Sterne overturns the whole structure of contemporary anthropology: instead of offering a natural explanation of the self, it now makes the self inaccessible. Thus the theory of the humours achieves two things: it throws the self into the foreground by focusing upon its nature; and it nullifies definition of the self by showing the impenetrability of that nature.

The theory of the humours is marred both for Tristram and the homunculus by an all-important lacuna – namely, how they are combined. What, then, could be more natural than to refer to a philosophy which had pondered this very problem and in so doing heralded the age of Enlightenment? From the very beginning *Tristram Shandy* comes to grips with the ideas of John Locke, which indeed permeate the whole novel, and which we shall be discussing in some detail. Mother Shandy's connection of her marital duties with the winding of the clock is an early illustration of Locke's association of ideas; here, as elsewhere, the idiosyncrasy is infuriating for the partner, but it is also responsible for the manner in which Tristram's body fluids are mixed. It is, therefore, scarcely surprising that he regards such a mechanism as being the cause of his misfortunes.

Against the background of Locke's philosophy, the self

seems almost the embodiment of chance, and so it becomes very doubtful whether the desired interplay between the humours can be brought under control. In seeking the conditions of his beginnings, Tristram is forced to recognise the impossibility of ever finding them. And yet, with the theory of the humours and the association of ideas he has invoked the broadest possible range of both anthropological and epistemological modes of comprehension, only to realise that the best they can offer him is awareness of the incomprehensibility of his origin.

The opening of the novel can, however, also point in another direction. The theory of the humours and the association of ideas are both overarching frameworks, whose evident inadequacy spotlights something new to be revealed to the reader – namely, the self referring to itself. As itself it can only be manifested through a striking double perspective: viewing prevailing frames of reference, it devalues them; and viewed *from* these frames of reference, it functions as their negation. By doing both simultaneously, it resists any cognitive definition and so distances itself from the expected function of the characters in the eighteenth-century novel. Thus it cannot be a 'flat character', let alone an allegorical one, and even if their predictable reactions make Walter and Toby seem like 'flat characters' (see Forster, *Aspects of the Novel*, pp. 65–79), the resemblance is only structural, as they nullify the concomitant function by standing for something impenetrable.

The circumstantial opening of the novel highlights its basic procedural mode. All facts presented at the outset appear to relate to a beginning without, however, constituting one, since what is said points back to a conditionality which ceaselessly dwindles into unfathomableness. This is certainly not in line with the beginning as observed in the eighteenth-century novel. Therefore Tristram assures us in various passages throughout the narrative that these either are or could be a beginning. What emerges from such references is not so much *the* beginning, but rather the actual nature of beginnings. Soon after this factual opening, he announces:

. . . right glad I am that I have begun the history of myself in the way I have done; and that I am able to go on tracing everything in it, as Horace says, *ab Ovo*. Horace, I know, does not recommend this fashion altogether: But that gentleman is speaking only of an epic poem or a tragedy – (I forget which) . . . for in writing what I have set about, I shall confine myself neither to his rules, nor to any man's rules that ever lived. (I, 4, 12)

After Tristram has begun, he comments on his own beginning, and if he is referring here to common ground between himself and his reader, it is only in order to undermine that common ground and thus bring out the otherness of his own approach. He takes *ab ovo* in its quite literal sense, thereby exposing the artificiality of the conventional beginnings of novels, which under pretext of being a start are in fact no more than postulates laid down to ratify the end. Indeed the 'truthfulness' of this 'history of myself' is derived from the narrator's personal set of rules, since these can only be understood retrospectively as a pattern of interconnected ramifications, whereas prospectively they are always open and, therefore, unpredictable. Hindsight confirms the veracity by exposing the unpredictability of connections that have now become clear. It follows, then, that this story can only be written, as it were, backwards, since the aim is to bring light into the dense thicket of diversifications. History can, of course, only be written from the standpoint of an end, but is not birth itself an end, and indeed is not conception the end of that which preceded it and of that which at the time was unforeseeable? Where does one begin the beginning? Sterne's narrator is totally conscious of this problem, and so all his beginnings are riddled with reservations and must, therefore, remain abortive.

Even when the narrative is nearing its end, the talk is once again of a beginning. Chapter 40 of Book 6 opens with the remark:

I am now beginning to get fairly into my work; and by the help of a vegetable diet, with a few of the cold seeds, I make no doubt but I shall be able to go on with my uncle Toby's story, and my own, in a tolerable straight line. (VI, 40, 384f.)

Now if this effort to go in a straight line is to be a genuine beginning, then such a beginning will run directly counter to the method Tristram has practised so far. For linear narration is precisely what Tristram has hitherto regarded as a 'minus function', i.e. the deliberate omission of an expected technique (for the term see J. Lotman, *Die Struktur literarischer Texte*, pp. 144ff., 207 and 267), as can be seen from the lines with which he depicts the wanderings of his previous volumes. One of the main reasons why he deliberately avoids linearity is that it can reveal nothing about the beginning but a great deal about the end, and the beginning that Tristram is searching for should not

be determined by being the beginning of an end. Straight lines
adumbrate teleology, and indeed Tristram points to a few
variations on the teleological theme:

This *right line*, – the pathway for Christians to walk in! Say divines – –
The emblem of moral rectitude! says *Cicero* – – The *best line*! say
cabbage planters – is the shortest line, says Archimedes, which can be
drawn from one given point to another.   (VI, 40, 386)

If straight lines prefigure journeys to commonplace goals,
what, then, might be the goal of Tristram's history? The answer
is yet another question, which Tristram puts to his reader at the
end of the chapter:

Pray can you tell me, – that is, without anger, before I write my chapter
upon straight lines – by what mistake – who told them so – or how it
has come to pass, that you men of wit and genius have all along
confounded this line with the line of GRAVITATION?

(VI, 40, 386)

For men of wit and genius all events gravitate towards an
end, which signals 'perfection' even when it is just a matter of
arranging cabbages in the right order, and Tristram's history
has already reminded readers of the literal meaning of
'GRAVITATION': it is a continual fall, whether it be the sash-
window falling upon his genitals, or the hot chestnut falling
down 'into that aperture of Phutatorius's breeches' (IV, 22,
261), or the splintering stone falling on Toby's groin. If the
illustrious intellects mistake this fall for the straight line –
straightness indeed being a fundamental feature of the free fall –
then it follows that their linear teleology will not gravitate
towards the fulfilment of a goal, but will itself constitute a free
fall whose consequences and implications will be unpredictable.
In his life, Tristram has plenty of experience of the straight-
lined free fall, whose description does not strike him altogether
as a bad idea for getting his story going. However, the
gravitation he describes does not suggest a teleological movement, but the linearity of a free fall, the very nature of which
excludes the certainty of where it may end. Therefore, what the
gravitational line will hit is as uncertain as the actual beginning
that Tristram is trying to catch hold of. This is why his attempts
at last to find a straight line may just as well constitute a
beginning for him. But if his aim is to find a straight line, then
the lines themselves *are* the purpose, and so cannot *have* a

purpose. The side effect of this – which is no doubt deliberate on Sterne's part – is that the linear technique of narration as practised in the eighteenth century is shown up in all its interest-governed conditionality.

Just as the 'straight line' discussion centres on conventional narrative expectations, so too does another of Tristram's attempts to get started. After the death of his brother Bobby, Tristram becomes

heir apparent to the Shandy family – and it is from this point properly that the story of my LIFE and my OPINIONS sets out; with all my hurry and precipitation I have but been clearing the ground to raise the building – and such a building do I foresee it will turn out, as never was planned, and as never was executed, since Adam. In less than five minutes I shall have thrown my pen into the fire, and the little drop of thick ink which is left remaining at the bottom of my inkhorn after it – I have but half a score of things to do in the time – I have a thing to name – a thing to lament – a thing to hope – a thing to promise, and a thing to threaten – I have a thing to suppose – a thing to declare – a thing to conceal – a thing to choose, and a thing to pray for.

(IV, 32, 273f.)

So far his search for the beginning has had birth as its starting-point, but now it is another man's death that appears to be the beginning of Tristram's story; and just as birth staggered its way back into preconditional ramifications, now death explodes his story into a multiplicity of possibilities, the simultaneous realisation of which transforms the temporal sequence of his story into a space-like instantaneity – whose singularity has never before been attempted in human history. This could imply that Sterne, as the architect of the transformation, is vying with the Creator – a commonplace idea which was on the rise in the eighteenth century.

As the heir apparent, Tristram slips into the role of a hero who, according to eighteenth-century narrative conventions, was meant to represent norms and values to be tested by multifarious events and finally ratified through the continuity of his story. And indeed Sterne does not dispute this representative role; on the contrary, the renewed beginning of Tristram's story would seem to stress this expectation Tristram is now the representative of the house of Shandy. But what characterises this house is not the norms and values of the eighteenth-century world picture; reigning in this house is the singularity of the self, whose eccentric history must run counter to all existing guidelines as none of them is able to capture it.

There are several more examples of different beginnings, but none of them go any further towards solving the basic problem of making a start. Worth mentioning is the foreword, which stands not at the beginning but in the middle of the book. Another point to note is the fact that the first book ends twenty-three years before Tristram's birth, and the last five years before, the latter actually concluding with a remark made by Yorick, who had already died in the first book. Thus, the end often seems like a beginning, and the beginning often marks an end.

What, then, can be the purpose of all these beginnings? We have already noted the difference between *Tristram Shandy* and other eighteenth-century novels, which began either *ab ovo* or rushed *in medias res*, in order to endow with verisimilitude what Congreve called 'an Unity of Contrivance' (see *The Complete Works* I, p. 112) as the hallmark of narrative. In comparison, the factual opening of *Tristram Shandy* seems artificial, although it sets out to investigate a natural event. What Sterne does is to use an evident 'Contrivance' in order to expose as artificial the suppositions behind the apparent naturalness of the conventional beginnings of novels. The unmasking of that strategy constitutes a purpose in itself; yet as Sterne must also find a beginning, his book is subject to problems that are comparable to those whose solutions he is seeking to undermine. The opening of *Tristram Shandy* could, therefore, not confine itself to being just a new variation on how to start. Instead, as only one of several beginnings, it highlights the fact that all beginnings are geared to a presupposed outcome, which they are meant to lead up to. A multiplicity of beginnings throws this hidden interconnection into relief, thus exposing the beginning as a retroactive patterning in accordance with the result intended.

The fact that Tristram's life story has no beginning, and that beginnings defy exploration, does not mean that the matter is simply allowed to rest. On the contrary, the more the beginning resists capture, the greater is the effort to overcome its recalcitrance. Thus, the narrator keeps approaching Tristram's life from different directions in the hope of pinning down its starting-point. But Sterne has also endowed the narrator with insight into the fact that none of his possible beginnings can ever be equated with *the* beginning, and so each individual attempt is counteracted by its consequences which, in turn, undermine its aspirations to be *the* solution. This gives rise to an ambivalence, which is in itself extremely revealing. The very fact that beginnings elude one's grasp triggers the drive to capture them, the cost, however, being that a state of validity is withheld from the solution provided. Therefore, all these solutions are nothing but images of how beginnings can be pictured.

This development is already hinted at in the title of the novel. *The Life and Opinions of Tristram Shandy, gentleman* suggests that these will be opinions inspired by and passed upon life. But according to Dr Johnson, opinion is '*Perswasion* of the mind, without proof and certain knowledge', and he quotes Ben Jonson in support of this definition: '*Opinion* is a light, vain, crude and imperfect thing, settled in the imagination, but never arriving at the understanding, there to obtain the tincture of reason' (Johnson, *Dictionary*). This contemporary definition of the word is underlined by the motto on the title page of *Tristram Shandy*, which stems from Epictetus and reads: 'It is not actions, but opinions concerning actions, which disturb men.'

The opinions to be expressed on life are ideas which can never cover what they are meant to embrace. In this way the implied author shades into the narrator, who thus speaks with two voices – not because he describes his life and expresses views on it, but because all his utterances are permeated with the knowledge that life exceeds its depiction and can, as it were, only be theatrically staged. The beginning is one example of this, and the characters are another.

Sterne has imbued his novel with consciousness that narration is the conceivability of the otherwise elusive, and at the same time he shows clearly that this insight leads not to resignation, but to a process of stimulating the reader's imagination. What has constantly been referred to as self-reflexivity in Sterne has its roots in his awareness of the ineradicable difference between the given object and its representation. This is why narrative for him is a matter of staging and not of mimesis. This is all the more evident as he tells of that which cannot be imitated – first, the beginning, and then the subjectivity of the self. Nevertheless, he also shows that those areas of life which are impenetrable to cognition must be narrated, because they can only become accessible to us as staged ideas.

2 Subjectivity discovered through Locke's philosophy

Since the narrator knows that his narrative is a form of staging, the novel does not need to convey its truths by creating illusions. Freed from the necessity to establish verisimilitude, it can concentrate its attentions on discovery. This exploratory movement is paramount in *Tristram Shandy*, which invades the given world far more radically than conventional novels or even those pretending to portray reality. This intervention relates to prevailing interpretations of the world, which in general are not reproduced so much as exposed by uncovering the problems they failed to cope with. Every novel has its extratextual fields of reference, upon which it imposes a perspectival slant, which both exhibits and overshoots the existing organisation by the very act of reproducing it. This lies at the root of the novel's world-relatedness, for instead of merely reflecting reality, it exposes reality to view.

One of *Tristram Shandy's* central fields of reference is the philosophy of Locke, which was the cornerstone of eighteenth-century English thought and which, by establishing the empirical tradition, provided a revolutionary impulse for Continental philosophy. About a hundred years after Locke's *Essay Concerning Human Understanding*, Kant wrote in his introduction to *Critique of Pure Reason*:

That all our knowledge begins with experience there can be no doubt. For how is it possible that the faculty of cognition should be awakened into exercise otherwise than by means of objects which affect our senses, and partly of themselves produce representations, partly rouse our powers of understanding into activity, to compare, to connect, or to separate these, and so to convert the raw material of our sensuous impressions into a knowledge of objects, which is called experience?

(p. 25)

This sentence summarises the principles of cognition developed in the second book of Locke's *Essay*, which describes the acquisition of knowledge from experience. Locke's philosophy was the dominant thought system of the eighteenth century, for it promised a solution to the problem – increasingly urgent from the Renaissance onwards – of man's self-preservation. Everything we can know 'we can have only by *sensation*' (Locke, *Essay* IV, 11, 1). '. . . For we cannot act anything but by our faculties, nor talk of knowledge itself but by the help of those faculties which are fitted to apprehend even what knowledge is'

(IV, 11, 3). This is an extremely comforting assurance, whose value is not diminished by the fact that we cannot know everything. 'For our faculties being suited not to the full extent of being, nor to a perfect, clear, comprehensive knowledge of things free from all doubt and scruple, but to the preservation of us in whom they are, and accommodated to the use of life: they serve to our purpose well enough if they will but give us certain notice of those things which are convenient or inconvenient to us' (IV, 11, 8). In spite of the limitations of our cognitive faculties, their capabilities are sufficient to guarantee the acquisition of certainty necessary to sustain our existence. What matters is not the perfectibility of our knowledge, but the possibility it gives us to preserve ourselves.

Locke's epistemology is unmistakably pervaded by anthropological concerns, which at times underpin the whole process of cognition and are invoked when principles of cognition can no longer be grasped analytically. This interdependence between epistemology and anthropology grows from their common root in experience, which is not only the source of knowledge but also its guarantee.

Knowledge then seems to me to be nothing but *the perception of the connexion and agreement, or disagreement and repugnancy, of any of our ideas.* In this alone it consists. Where this perception is, there is knowledge; and where it is not, there, though we may fancy, guess, or believe, yet we always come short of knowledge.   (IV, 1, 2)

Since knowledge arises from the combination of 'simple ideas' – impinging on the mind from outside – it can be increased, simultaneously promising successful self-preservation by developing the human faculties. This link had a powerful attraction for the age of Enlightenment, not because a new objective was to replace an old one, but because self-development now appeared as the necessary offshoot of self-preservation.

The significance of this natural explanation of man's cognitive faculty can be gauged from the fact that empiricism, as the dominant thought system of the eighteenth century, relegated Christian supernaturalism to the level of a sub-system, to be observed in the natural explanation of the Revelation, ranging from Locke's *Reasonableness of Christianity* (1695) through John Toland's *Christianity not Mysterious* (1696) to Matthew Tindal's *Christianity as old as the Creation* (1730).

But systems as problem-solving organisations produce or leave behind something which they are unable to tackle, and it is on this residue of Locke's system that *Tristram Shandy* sets its sights. Through the circumstances of his birth, the narrator feels himself to be a victim of Locke's cognitive premises:

namely, that, from an unhappy association of ideas which have no connection in nature, it so fell out at length that my poor mother could never hear the said clock wound up, – but the thoughts of some other things unavoidably popped into her head, – and *vice versa*: – which strange combination of ideas the sagacious Locke, who certainly understood the nature of these things better than most men, affirms to have produced more wry actions than all other sources of prejudice whatsoever.   (I, 4, 13)

Locke would certainly not have contradicted such an association of ideas, for he distinguished between '*real ideas* . . . [which] have a foundation in nature' and '*Fantastical* or *chimerical* [ideas] . . . as have no foundation in nature, nor have any conformity with that reality of being to which they are tacitly referred, as to their archetypes' (II, 30, 1). However clear the distinction may seem, though, 'this doctrine imposes a terrible burden of proof on Locke' (Traugott, *Tristram Shandy's World*, p. 34). For the complex ideas are brought about by way of *Reflection*, and so are products of the human mind, of which we learn that 'the mind of man uses some kind of liberty in forming those complex *ideas*' (Locke, II, 30, 3). If intellectual freedom plays a role in associating ideas, how does this affect the regulative function of archetypes, which seek to restrict such freedom? This is the problem that Sterne latches on to, offering an answer to the question Locke appeared unable to tackle.

Locke rejected Descartes' innate ideas, which did not permit any increase of knowledge through their combination, and so found himself compelled to assume the existence of archetypes in order to prevent combinations from getting out of hand. While Descartes assumed the reliability of cognition to be guaranteed by divine decree, Locke saw '*experience* and history' as the only 'way of *getting* and *improving our knowledge*' (IV, 12, 10). The archetypes he postulates are a sort of remnant of a 'concept of reality' which Blumenberg calls 'guaranteed reality' – i.e. preordained by God – while Locke's claim that knowledge is to be gained from experience shows that reality must be for him the 'result of a realisation, as a successively self-constituting reliability, never achieving final or absolute consistency' (Hans Blumenberg, 'Wirklichkeitsbegriff und Möglichkeit des Romans', pp. 11f.).

Locke's theory of cognition marks an apex of epistemology in the modern world. He still refrained from viewing the archetypes heuristically, for he considered their basis to be in nature; at the same time, however, the human mind is endowed with a freedom that can escape from the boundaries laid down by the archetypes. The association of ideas would be pre-determined if it were regulated only by the archetypes; and if it emerged solely from the mind's faculty of combination, it would be unlimited.

This is the point at which Sterne latches on to the Lockean system. His first example shows the association of ideas being determined by a habit. The habit of linking the winding of the clock with the sexual act functions like a Lockean archetype, without actually being one, for its basis is not in nature. Its origin can, therefore, only lie in the human mind, which regulates the association of ideas. Habit, then, is just a manifestation of this regulator, whose effectiveness is continually confirmed by experience. Thus, Sterne simplifies and thereby clarifies a situation that had become increasingly complex in the Lockean system. The association of ideas did indeed take place through the workings of the human mind, but as a wax tablet the mind was passive, whereas it was active as an instrument of reflection. The combination of ideas occurred sometimes through given archetypes and sometimes through simple modes – both of which had their foundations in nature – but sometimes also through 'mixed modes' as well as through the free associations of the mind, and the two latter agents had no guarantee from nature. Furthermore, Locke talked of the human mind as if it were a collective substance, in which every human being participated almost in the same sense in which Plato had conceived of it, in consequence of which failed associations are due only to an individual's incompetence – indicating that he is out of his mind – but by no means to the assumed structure of the mind in general.

But what *is* the decisive impulse behind the association of ideas? Sterne's answer is: the human self, which he considered a point of reference for the association of ideas, thereby uncovering the blind spot in the Lockean system. Of course, in terms of cognitive theory this discovery has ruinous consequences: if the association of ideas is guided by the habits of the self, then it means goodbye to the acquisition of knowledge through experience. For as long as habit prevails, it sets up entrenched expectations which would have to be thwarted if experience were to ensue. But the latter process also had its problematical side in Locke. As long as archetypes, simple modes or even God were the decisive factors in the association, their very constancy as regulators produced predictable rather than unpredictable combinations. Experience, however, requires the unpredictable, since experience must by definition entail something new. Locke was also aware of this problem, which is why he always provided anthropological compensations when his epistemological theory ran into difficulties. Sterne makes the self the pivot of associations that never occurred to Locke, and thus he radicalises the blind spot in the latter's latent anthropology.

The price of this radicalisation is the loss of cognitive guarantees, for the self is now thrown back upon itself. It takes on its individual shape by means of its habits, which guide the association of ideas. Since habits, however, are acquired, they cannot be the origin of the self. When the family are awaiting the birth of Tristram, and Dr Slop is confronted with the difficulty of untying the many knots on his instrument bag, we read:

Great wits jump: for the moment Dr. Slop cast his eyes upon his bag (which he had not done till the dispute with my uncle Toby about midwifery put him in mind of it), – the very same thought occurred. – 'Tis God's mercy, quoth he (to himself), that Mrs. Shandy has had so bad a time of it; – else she might have been brought to bed seven times told, before one half of these knots could have got untied. – But here, you must distinguish – the thought floated only in Dr. Slop's mind, without sail or ballast to it, as a simple proposition; millions of which, as your Worship knows, are every day swimming quietly in the middle of the thin juice of a man's understanding, without being carried backwards or forwards, till some little gusts of passion or interest drive them to one side. (III, 9, 135)

Here Tristram is alluding to the motivation that underlies the association of ideas. Passions, interests, and often sheer chance drive different ideas together which – as perceptual data received from outside – lie dormant in the human mind until they are activated by some subjective impulse. Habits are the consolidated forms of these impulses, which sometimes spring from the most singular motivation.

Motivation as the origin of the association of ideas is scarcely touched on by Locke, for the successful combinations he deals with come about by regulators rooted in nature. This is why in Locke it sometimes seems as if the mind is merely a parade-ground for factors of cognition given by nature. In order to do justice to the mind's inherent gift for combination, Locke has to have recourse to metaphors as explanations for the resultant links. Perhaps the most important of these is the 'train of ideas', through which he seeks to pin down the concept of succession as a condition for the complex idea of time. This has the advantage of an almost non-existent content while at the same time being backed by and thus coinciding with experience. In this context, as in others, Sterne radicalises the Lockean concept, extracting the figurative element from the metaphor and then offering an idea of what could motivate the succession:

In swims CURIOSITY, beckoning to her damsels to follow – they dive into the centre of the current – FANCY sits musing upon the bank, and with her eyes following the stream, turns straws and bulrushes into masts and bowsprits. – And DESIRE, with vest held up to the knee in one hand, snatches at them, as they swim by her, with the other –.
(VIII, 5, 440f.)

What motivates the association of ideas eludes the grasp of an analytic approach. In so far as Locke was aware of this, he used metaphors to get round the difficulties thrown up by analytic argumentation. Sterne focuses on these metaphors in order to find out what they are meant to illustrate. By parading human impulses and faculties as allegories, he reveals the figurative nature of the metaphor. Each of these personifi-cations seems to be governed by a different motive which, no doubt, sets the association of ideas in motion, but – owing to its metaphorical nature – eclipses the explanation of that which causes the link-up. Now, if the roots of combinations are so manifold, their origins could be nothing but subjective, as is highlighted by the surprising links established. There is simply no knowing why Mother Shandy associates the sexual act with winding up the clock, why Walter Shandy connects almost all events with the premisses of scholastic rhetoric, or Uncle Toby thinks of everything – even love – in terms of fortifications. These associations springing from habit throw the self of the characters into relief, and as the origins of the habit are equally idiosyncratic, subjectivity is spotlighted as the core of the self. This conception runs through the novel and is virulent right up to the end: 'A man cannot dress, but his ideas get clothed at the same time' (IX, 13, 502). With the motivation inexplicable yet present in its manifestation, this origin of association serves as a schema to translate the self into terms of impenetrable subjectivity, which eludes capture by suspending all frames of reference. Since subjectivity precedes the efforts to grasp it cognitively, it turns into a propellant for the urgent desire to come to grips with it. What cannot be explained has to be staged. Only in this way can subjectivity escape from the Scylla of referential definition and the Charybdis of being pinned down to definite origins. For in both cases it would no longer be itself.

From this vantage-point the various beginnings of *Tristram Shandy* come to full fruition. They are beginnings in so far as they serve to open up situations for a theatrically staged subjectivity, which in its various performances reveals a cast as massive as its impenetrability.

3   Locke's philosophy as a pattern of communication

In this respect Lockean philosophy is transformed into a pattern of communication, which serves to highlight the subjectivity of human nature as the deformation of the association of ideas. Sterne based his approach on a dominant thought system of his time because he could take its familiarity for granted, and thus turn it into a suitable medium through which to translate subjectivity for his reading public. To this end he uncovers the weaknesses of Locke's philosophy wherever cognitive theory and anthropology shore each other up: either the self is the pivot for the association of ideas, in which case basic premises of epistemology fall by the wayside, or the association follows given premises of cognition, in which case the system requires no anthropological patches. According to Locke: 'If our knowledge were altogether necessary, all men's knowledge would not only be alike, but every man would know all that is knowable; and if it were wholly voluntary, some men so little regard or value it that they would have extreme little, or none at all' (IV, 13, 1). But as for the relationship between necessity and freedom as guidelines for the acquisition of knowledge, this lay beyond the scope of conceptualisation, for Lockean empiricism knows no transcendental stances. It is the territory that Locke had to ignore which Sterne now explores by anchoring the association of ideas in the motivation of the self. The gap in Locke's system is filled by the subjectivity of the self. The process, however, is an insidious one, for it offers no direct criticism of the system; instead it simply takes it and presents it literally. For subjectivity is as ungraspable as the source of knowledge gained through combining ideas. What was analytically inaccessible to Locke, Sterne presents as the singularity of subjectivity.

The transformation of Locke's philosophy into a pattern of communication for the newly-discovered subjectivity has certain side-effects, highlighting the artistic techniques of Sterne's encroachment on his external fields of reference. He conspicuously refrains from negating Locke's norms of cognition. The negation of norms would automatically require their replacement by others in opposition to those under attack. But Sterne in fact applies Locke's norms, in a manner that follows them through to their logical conclusions. In doing so he brings to the fore the claim inherent in all norms – namely, to be universal regulators. All of them carry the assumption that what they regulate is brought into complete order. Consequently Sterne takes the association of ideas at their face value, which enables the human mind not only to select data received from the outside world, but also to combine them. And he finds that, since there are no innate ideas – as Descartes had conceived them – in the human mind, the latter will perform its acts of combination in accordance with the freedom at its disposal: the result is the emergence of subjectivity, which in view of its eccentricity leads to a self-imposed isolation.

This seemingly disastrous effect, however, makes it clear that the association of ideas as a norm of cognition is not an integral component of reality (which it could not be, for it has to organise reality). Only when reality is conceptualised as 'guaranteed reality' can norms also be its component parts, as borne out by the innate ideas of Descartes. If reality, however, is conceived as a process of realisation constantly emanating from the knowledge generated by the association of ideas, then experience and the norms that process it split apart, which makes all guiding principles increasingly idiosyncratic in proportion to their claim to universal validity. Thus the central norm of Locke's theory of cognition unexpectedly turns into the *hobby-horse* whose limitations are all too apparent in comparison with the reality it tries to cover.

By making incursions into empirical philosophy as his field of reference, Sterne was able to achieve several things at the same time. First, by uncovering an agent responsible for the association of ideas, which was certainly not in Locke's orbit, he transformed the latter's system into a communicative structure to render subjectivity conceivable for a public whose reading convention made them expect the hero of a novel to be the carrier of a message. Subjectivity is, therefore, not to be mistaken as a representation of the Lockean system; instead, it destroys this frame of reference in order to bring out its singularity. Secondly, this destruction is wrought by taking the cognitive norms at their face value, thus exposing what they had glossed over – namely, the difference between norm and reality, in consequence of which the claim of the norm to be a universal explanation either appears fictitious or it turns its defenders into one-track dogmatists. Such an exposure of Lockean norms is rather akin to the ideas of Hume, who considered all concepts to be nothing but 'fictions of the mind' (see *A Treatise of Human Nature*, pp. 37, 48, 65, 197, 220, 254, 259 and 493). This was not meant to discredit them so much as to establish their status, which was characterised by the fact that they were different from nature since they were devised in order to conceptualise nature. In this connection it is revealing that Hume considered *Tristram Shandy* to be 'the best book that has been writ by any Englishman these thirty years' (see *Letters*, p. 269).

The categorical difference between norm and reality, which is the common ground between Sterne and Hume's critique of the inherited tradition, is of major significance for the topography of the conventional eighteenth-century novel. Here reality served as a backdrop against which the hero had to prove himself, whereas in Sterne subjectivity is exposed to a world which is immeasurably greater than anything that can be covered by men's ideas. If the characters hold fast to their personal ways of combining ideas, mistakenly identifying them with reality, the result is confusion and catastrophe. Thus the world ceases to be a setting made to measure for the hero and his virtues, and instead it becomes an abyss which the characters have dug out for themselves through their commitment to their own association of ideas. This brings to the fore a third element that Sterne extrapolates from Locke's system: he uses it for character portrayal. All the figures ride their own *hobby-horses*, which are the expression of their unmistakable singularity. This is a very special artifice of Sterne's. (1) While the characters are uniformly conceived in accordance with their association of ideas, the sources and motives of their respective combinations make them branch out into a variety of totally distinct figures beside whom the conventional message-bearing characters of the eighteenth-century novel seem like pale shadows. (2) By cutting his figures to the Lockean pattern, Sterne is able to dispense with the representational function and thus present subjectivity as itself. (3) In taking the association of ideas at face value – in accordance with Locke's conviction that there was no way to reach behind it – Sterne conceived it as an individual signature of the subject's self-referentiality.

These three strands tend to overlap in *Tristram Shandy*, and on their respective dominance will depend whether it is the representation or evaluation of subjectivity that occupies the foreground. Indeed these aspects, despite the fact that they may point in different directions, are never separated from one another, as it is their interplay that renders subjectivity conceivable. They continually reflect back upon Lockean philosophy, exposing it as a sort of spelling aid, or a theoretical naïvety, or a plethora of forms for character portrayal. The resultant implicit criticism, however, is not meant to put the philosophy right; for the most part, Sterne uncovers its weakness in order to give shape to the themes that this novel is to develop. The recoding of the thought system aims not to destroy it but to exploit those implications that had remained hidden so long as the system was understood on terms set by itself. The fact that Sterne made Locke's empiricism into his central field of reference is an indication of the innovative character of represented subjectivity, for only by deconstructing the prevailing code could he draw attention to and establish the necessary conditions for its conceivability.

4   Manic subjectivity

What are the basic elements of this newly-thematised subjectivity? Traces of its characteristic features are already to be found in Locke, who despite his preoccupation with regulative principles was not unaware of the fact that subjective factors were also operative in the combination of ideas. He makes it quite clear, however, that these factors are pathological, for he designates them as 'madness' (II, 33, 3). A striking example of such aberrations is the following:

. . . there is another connexion of *ideas* wholly owing to chance or custom: *ideas*, that in themselves are not at all of kin, come to be so united in some men's minds that it is very hard to separate them, they always keep in company, and the one no sooner at any time comes into the understanding but its associate appears with it; and if they are more than two which are thus united, the whole gang, always inseparable, show themselves together.   (II, 33, 5)

By this reckoning Walter Shandy and Uncle Toby must be counted amongst the madmen, for not only does this description apply perfectly to them, but they also follow the example of the man who 'so cements those two *ideas* together that he makes them almost one' (II, 33, 11). But instead of diagnosing this madness, Locke is more concerned with ratifying his description of this process:

I shall be pardoned for calling it by so harsh a name as *madness*, when it is considered that opposition to reason deserves that name and is really madness; and there is scarce a man so free from it but that, if he should always on all occasions argue or do as in some cases he constantly does, would not be thought fitter for Bedlam than civil conversation.
                                                                (II, 33, 4)

The reference to Bedlam – the colloquial abbreviation for Bethlehem Hospital – is in itself revealing, for this institution, founded in 1547, was a lunatic asylum that was run not for the benefit of its patients, but as an exhibition where the public paid to see the inmates on show. Even in the early eighteenth century, Tom Brown in his *London Amusement* was still recommending a visit to Bedlam 'for any gentleman, disposed for a *touch* of the times' (Rousseau, 'Science', p. 181). Locke's allusion also occurs elsewhere in a similar context (II, 11, 13), and by madness he clearly means incurable disease, for awareness of possible cures did not arise till the mid-eighteenth century. The traces of subjectivity to be found in the association of ideas are related, then, to a peculiarity that is regarded as incurable madness. The prevailing frame of reference insists that whoever opposes reason cuts himself off from the rational community. Subjectivity as 'insanity' – which appears to be its first historically traceable definition – denotes its severance from all relations by plunging itself into isolation. Its so-called madness becomes apparent as it subjugates overarching ordering systems – such as the association of ideas – to the disclosure of its singularity, in consequence of which conventional and traditional standards are virtually turned upside down.

This seemingly paradoxical situation is exacerbated by the fact that singularity as the keynote of subjectivity does not reveal what conditions its uniqueness. Manifestations do not explain the base which they have adumbrated, and 'oddity' is too collective a qualification to enable the individualisation of subjectivity to be grasped. How, then, is singularity to be differentiated? The outline of an answer is to be found on the level of the characters. Walter and Toby provide a starting-point, and this undergoes an important modification through Tristram and Yorick.

Walter and Toby appear to be the most likely candidates for Locke's Bedlam, even though they are the characters most closely tied to Locke's philosophy. Does this mean that ultimately such a philosophy leads to madness? At a vital moment leading up to the birth, Walter asks the people assembled in the living-room of Shandy Hall how it could be that since the arrival of Dr Slop and Obadiah only two hours and ten minutes have elapsed, although it seems to him like an eternity. The question is, of course, meant to be rhetorical but Toby at once chips in with the all-important catch-phrase: ''Tis owing, entirely . . . to the succession of our ideas.' Quite put out by the fact that Toby has stolen his thunder, Walter asks him what he knows about it. 'No more than my horse', is the rejoinder. And now Walter is in his element:

Gracious heaven! cried my father, looking upwards, and clasping his two hands together, – there is a worth in thy honest ignorance, brother Toby; – 'twere almost a pity to exchange it for a knowledge. – But I'll tell thee. – To understand what *time* is aright, without which we never can comprehend *infinity*, insomuch as one is a portion of the other, – we ought seriously to sit down and consider what idea it is we have of *duration*, so as to give a satisfactory account how we came by it. – What is that to anybody? quoth my uncle Toby. *For if you will turn your eyes inwards upon your mind,* continued my father, *and observe attentively, you will perceive, brother, that whilst you and I are talking together, and thinking and smoking our pipes; or whilst we receive successively ideas in our minds; we know that we do exist, and so we estimate the existence or the continuation of the existence of ourselves, or anything else commensurate to the succession of any ideas in our minds, the duration of ourselves, or any such other thing coexisting with our thinking, – and so according to that preconceived.* – You puzzle me to death, cried my Uncle Toby. – 'Tis owing to this, replied my father, that in our computations of *time*, we are so used to minutes, hours, weeks, and months . . . that 'twill be well, if in time to come, *the succession of our*

ideas be of any use or service to us at all. Now, whether we observe it or
no, continued my father, in every sound man's head, there is a regular
succession of ideas of one sort or other, which follow each other in
train just like – A train of artillery? said my uncle Toby. – A train of a
fiddlestick! – quoth my father, – which follow and succeed one another
in our minds at certain distances, just like the images in the inside of a
lantern turned round by the heat of a candle. – I declare, quoth my
uncle Toby, mine are like a smokejack. – Then, brother Toby, I have
nothing more to say to you upon the subject, said my father.

(III, 18, 152ff.)

This is an almost exact echo of Locke, and indeed Sterne said in
a footnote 'Vid. Locke'. But instead of this guaranteeing
mutual understanding, we have a complete breakdown of
communication which would undoubtedly make the two
brothers – judging by Locke's criteria – potential inmates of
Bedlam. If Walter does seem somewhat unhinged, it is not
because he bonds together disparate ideas, but because he is
obsessed with the belief that Locke's philosophy is right and
that it can be applied as a universal explanation.

Thus the Lockean concept simply becomes a means whereby
subjectivity may be conceived and presented; at the same time
the character is freed from any taint of insanity, because he
follows so scrupulously the association of ideas. Anyone so
possessed by the correctness of Locke's cognitive premises
could not possibly be mad. The resultant obsession, which
typifies both Walter and Toby – though along completely
different lines – is quite unlike what Locke would have
envisaged. The only element of madness lies in the fact that the
Shandy brothers do not regard the breakdown of their
communication as a problem. An obsession that cannot be
broken becomes a mania indicating that the self lives in
inseparable communion with itself. This means that its references in and to the outside world – whether they be the
association of ideas or the artillery – are not perceived
cognitively, but are only present as integral components of the
character. The self expands into areas of reality, but these, in
turn, become so firmly incorporated in the self that any
difference between subject and object is erased. Singularity
consists in the very fact that the self selectively adapts reality,
and although it moves within the world, it does so in such a
manner that it never departs from itself. Obsession, then, is
unremitting resistance to any separation between self and

world, and it takes on a manic character because the separation is not even perceived when communication breaks down.

Mania itself, however, is also permeated by a difference which must not be allowed to penetrate into consciousness. Manic obsession entails at one and the same time a sundering of realities alien to the self, and a projection of the self on to the real world. To keep the magic spell of the mania from being broken, this dual process must not be allowed to filter into consciousness. This explains the contentment and indeed the cheerfulness that always mark the behaviour of the Shandy brothers, and even the misfiring of their conversation does not detract from the enjoyment they derive from their obsessions. They constantly offer cues by means of which they each ensure the incorporation into themselves of worlds that lie beyond them, thus providing experience of their own uninterrupted communion with themselves (cf. Hörhammer, *Die Formation des literarischen Humors*, pp. 61ff.).

This self-containment is reinforced by the fact that most of their lives are spent in the living-room at Shandy Hall, within whose narrow confines they are protected from any outside interference that might disturb the pleasure of their manic subjectivity. The only disturbances that do take place occur when they leave their enclave: Walter makes an unnecessary journey to London because of the phantom pregnancy of Mother Shandy, and Toby has an abortive love affair in the house of Widow Wadman. The parameters of Shandy Hall symbolise the boundaries within which the self can reside with itself.

The manic obsession which Locke would have dismissed as madness signifies subjectivity for Sterne. Mania and subjectivity seem each to condition the other, for mania acts as a blanket protection against any definition of what subjectivity is, and subjectivity in turn suppresses any attempt to split itself apart. Since the obsession is constantly under threat, it has to be maintained, even though the self may not be aware of the threat (for to be aware it would have to step out of itself).

5　Melancholic subjectivity

This state of affairs first becomes apparent on the level of the narrator. The very fact that Tristram intends to write his *Life* means that he is forced to face himself, or is at least confronted with traces of what he has been. As far as historical progress is concerned, he is not particularly successful (cf. Warning, *Illusion und Wirklichkeit in Tristram Shandy und Jacques le Fataliste*, pp. 15ff.). Not until Book 3 is he born, Book 4 contains his baptism, and Book 5 deals with the events of his fifth year. From then on he himself virtually ceases to be the subject of the narrative. It is now Toby with his imaginary military campaigns and his unsuccessful love affair who emerges as the 'hero' of Tristram's *Life*.

A basic reason for the slow progress of the story is Tristram's commitment to the principle of causality. 'My way is ever to point out to the curious, different tracts of investigation, to come at the first springs of the events I tell' (I, 21, 58), and here he knows himself to be in accordance with Locke's premises: 'viz. that a *cause* is that which makes any other thing, either simple *idea*, substance, or mode, begin to be, and an *effect* is that which had its beginning from some other thing: the mind finds no great difficulty to distinguish the several originals of things' (II, 26, 2). However, things do not appear to be so simple: it is plausible enough that one should assume causes, but how is one to know whether these in themselves are not the effects of previous causes? Tristram's concern with causality comes about through his attempt to explain to the reader the effect of Aunt Dinah's 'misfortune' – who 'was married and got with child by the coachman' (I, 21, 58) – on Walter and Toby. At one and the same time he confesses that: 'Why this cause of sorrow, therefore, was thus reserved for my father and uncle is undetermined by me. But how and in what direction it exerted itself, so as to become the cause of dissatisfaction between them after it began to operate, is what I am able to explain with great exactness' (I, 21, 58f.). Final causes can never be determined, for every attempt to grasp them will set in motion a *regressus ad infinitum*.

This remains paradigmatic for Tristram's life story, whose continuity is disrupted precisely because he tries painstakingly to observe the causality principle which ought in fact to guarantee coherence. If events are to be grasped by tracing them back to their causes, then Tristram's technique is thoroughly in accordance with Locke's premises of cognition, since the explanation of causes allows assessment of their effects. But disentangling the prehistory of events such as Tristram's birth leads inevitably into a narrative running backwards and threatening to lose itself entirely in the ramifications of its conditionality. And as the life that is supposed to be the subject of the narrative moves forwards, the principle of causality brings about an ever-widening gulf between the life and its rendering. Every event broadens out into its prehistory, whose unending ramifications make it impossible to discern a final cause, and therefore impossible to furnish the explanation for which it was invoked in the first place. This overload of prelife stories not only blocks the representation of Tristram's life, but also shows that his life eludes representation precisely because he is trying to grasp it through the principle of causality. Thus, the narrated life continually overshoots the principles and structures that are meant to capture it, making the universal claims of cognitive premises shrink to meagre partiality, and indicating by the recoded principle of causality that cognition can only trail further and further behind life.

As with the principle of association, that of causality, carried to its logical conclusions, is made to uncover what had hitherto remained hidden – namely, what happens between cause and effect, and how causes result in certain effects. The interplay operative in this relationship is not guided by any a priori principle, but is determined by the context within which it occurs. Thus, the narrative of a *Life* modelled according to the principle of causality is liable to grind to a halt, as all the presuppositions have to be traced before the circumstances they have produced can be dealt with. Now, as this interplay heads out into unfathomableness, Tristram as historian of his own life is bound to fail. But his failure is triumphant, in that it demonstrates that any bridging of the gap between cause and effect is sheer mythology – a pitfall which claims as victims both Locke and Walter Shandy in equal measure. Tristram, however, never loses sight of the gap which makes his life story so impossible to narrate.

The proliferating prehistories show that the link between cause and effect embodies a no man's land which Tristram is obliged to explore; at the same time, the forward movement of his life continually approaches open horizons which resist any attempt at structuring. Tristram himself is, therefore, situated at the point of intersection between what was and what is to be. The past is unfathomable, and the future is amorphous. What is left is simply the area between the two, and it is this that structures his history, of which he confesses:

. . . when a man sits down to write a history . . . he knows no more than his heels what lets and confounded hindrances he is to meet with in his way, – or what a dance he may be led, by one excursion or another, before all is over. Could a historiographer drive on his history, as a muleteer drives on his mule, – straight forwards – for instance, from Rome all the way to Loreto, without ever once turning his head aside either to the right hand or to the left, – he might venture to foretell you to an hour when he should get to his journey's end; – but the thing is, morally speaking, impossible: For, if he is a man of the least spirit, he will have fifty deviations from a straight line to make with this or that party as he goes along, which he can no ways avoid. He will have views and prospects to himself perpetually soliciting his eye, which he can no more help standing to look at than he can fly . . . In short, there is no end of it.   (I, 14, 36f.)

There is a huge difference between life and its rendering, which Tristram tries to narrow down in the act of writing. But his brain is as incapable as his heels of foreseeing in which direction he will be carried. Any attempt to look ahead would be mere speculation and would have nothing to do with the course of his life. Writing, however, requires something pre-given to be written about, and as the historian cannot catch up with his life, his writing pictures a life running ahead of him. But whenever pen and situation appear to touch one another, there is still the writing itself as the unbridgeable divide between the two, leaving only the option to write about writing. Thus, writing can never coincide with life, and facing up to this fact is a sign of the moral integrity of the historian. Indeed, this integrity will be violated whenever life and representation appear to coincide. Autobiographies which appear to 'achieve' this are nothing but illusory fulfilments of set purposes which substitute interpretations of life for life itself. By implication Tristram attacks the autobiographical form of the eighteenth-century novel precisely because it conceals the gap between life and representation, but on the other hand he does want to write about his life and not about the gap – a task which would itself turn into a purpose, thus imposing an illusory framework on his own writing. He wants to experience something about himself, and he would have no need of writing if he already knew who he was. Thus he has to remain aware of the difference between life and its interpretation – a difference which provides a continual incentive to write.

As a result of these countervailing trends, the narrative seems to be overloaded with details, one main reason for which is the fact that in searching for himself Tristram continually needs contact with different people whose varying viewpoints will best preserve him from imposing a one-sided interpretation on his own life. Ultimately he is forced to sacrifice the story line, which was still so integral to the eighteenth-century novel, and made life conceivable as a continuity. Instead he replaces one story by many, thus invalidating the claim of each one to be representative. The many stories serve to demonstrate that life vastly exceeds the confines of a story. In the fifty digressions mentioned, no matter what frame of reference is invoked, every one fails to provide an adequate guideline for the representation of a life. This applies as much to Locke's principle of causality as to the traditional narrative modes of the eighteenth-century novel, and the process even goes so far as to invalidate the constitutive conditions of narration – a fact that has led many Sterne critics to regard him not as a novelist any more, but as an artistic rhetorician (Traugott (1954) ch. 13).

Tristram's journey through his life leaves a trail of wreckage as far as its representation is concerned, evinced by the deformation to which nearly all the traditional narrative techniques have been subjected. Tristram, however, is writing in order to capture himself in and through his life. As the difference between Tristram's life and its narrative rendering can never be eliminated, all attempts at conceptualising it are dwarfed to mere views, mirroring a situational context, and so they lack authenticity. Tristram is unable to make himself tick. The best he can do is continually deconstruct the claims made by the manifestation of his life – claims inherent in the mere fact of his writing – to be representative of the whole, and this process is evident in his subversive approach to his history. Just as life always remains ahead of writing, so Tristram as an individual self is always ahead of his life; it is, therefore, as impossible for him as for his writing to be equated with his life. But by inscribing himself into the representation of his life, he makes the latter into a kind of mirror revealing his own relationship with himself. In this respect the apparent loss of any representative function – suggested by the wreckage of narrative conventions with which the novel is littered – is compensated by the narrative, for Tristram's *Life* shows that subjectivity consists in a relationship to oneself. The ineradicable difference between life and its representation there-

fore ceases to be a problem, since it is absorbed into the
relationship of the self with itself – a relationship that would be
undone if it were to develop into a solution. Tristram himself
talks of 'writing and publishing two volumes of my life every
year; – which, if I am suffered to go on quietly, and can make a
tolerable bargain with my bookseller, I shall continue to do as
long as I live' (I, 14, 37).

He will do so in full awareness that the life he writes about is
nothing but a mirroring of his relationship with himself, taking
on its form by destroying its own expected coherence, and so
the difference now internalised by splitting the self apart from
itself is bound to have repercussions on him. Tristram makes no
secret of this, when he writes that his book is not intended as an
attack on predestination, free-will or taxes, but:

If 'tis wrote against anything, – 'tis wrote, an' please your Worships,
against the spleen; in order, by a more frequent and a more convulsive
elevation and depression of the diaphragm, and the succussations of
the intercostal and abdominal muscles in laughter, to drive the *gall* and
other *bitter juices* from the gall bladder, liver, and sweetbread of his
Majesty's subjects, with all the inimicitious passions which belong to
them, down into their duodenums.   (IV, 22, 243)

To counteract the spleen and drive away the gall and bitter
juices simply means resisting the continual threat of melancholy. Writing does not aim at representing the self through its
own life, but at achieving a cure. The two intentions appear to
be quite different, but nevertheless they have a fundamental
link. Constantly chasing after one's life and deconstructing
oneself in the chase affects the temperament and leads to
melancholy. Writing, therefore, takes on a dual character: by
bringing about the ineluctable difference between self and life it
leads to melancholy which, in turn, is to be healed by the same
writing, which must mock at its own efforts by interspersing
seriousness with humour. Whatever forms of self-
representation Tristram sets up as a historian he undermines
with his own subjectivity, so that the writing always exhibits the
dual pattern of serious exposition followed by ridiculous
exposure. Offering one's own life story as an object of fun both
for oneself and others indicates a relationship of the self to the
self whose cognitive impenetrability is deliberately exposed to
laughter, which is the medicine Tristram would like to give his
readers, and he delivers it by way of example. In this respect

Tristram greatly resembles his author, for in the Dedication Sterne informs Pitt* that 'I live in a constant endeavour to fence against the infirmities of ill health, and other evils of life, by mirth; being firmly persuaded that every time a man smiles, – but much more so, when he laughs, that it adds something to this Fragment of Life' (Dedication, 7). Laughing away one's misery might be described as the content or substance of the self's relationship to itself, through which subjectivity is manifested.

6   Decentred subjectivity

Since subjectivity is marked by its peculiarity, it can only be fully demonstrated through its singular variations. And so Tristram is not content merely to unfold his own subjectivity, which while outstripping that of his father at the same time remains in the wake of the ideal projection embodied in Yorick. The latter advances to the forefront as the hero of the history, and indeed Tristram refers to him more than once as 'my Hero' (I, 12, 29; I, 10, 21). Those qualities that Tristram most admires are to be found in Yorick, who has the finest pedigree of any Sterne character. Not only does he descend in a direct line from Hamlet's 'king's chief Jester' (I, 11, 26), but he is also of equal rank with the comic genius of Don Quixote.

I have the highest idea of the spiritual and refined sentiments of this reverend gentleman, from this single stroke in his character, which I think comes up to any of the honest refinements of the peerless knight of La Mancha, whom, by the bye with all his follies, I love more, and would actually have gone further to have paid a visit to, than the greatest hero of antiquity.   (I, 10, 24)

Yorick, then, is the longed-for ideal, but even if he is a Don Quixote, he is distinguished from the 'locura' (madness) of that famous knight by the fact that he is acutely conscious of himself. He combines the craziness of the abstract idealist with the ambivalence of the Fool – an almost incredible combination. As Fool, he remains detached from everything, whereas as Don Quixote, he is always totally involved. And here we have a split that is quite different from that which characterises

* Statesman, who, according to Macaulay, made England the first country in the world.

Tristram. The latter is separated from his own life, whereas the split in Yorick takes place within himself, through the Fool's awareness and the idealist's blindness. When he rides his old horse through the district, it is because he would rather spend his money on the welfare of his community than on a new horse. His external appearance makes him an object of mockery, 'and . . . instead of giving the true cause, – he chose rather to join in the laugh against himself' (I, 10, 22). He much prefers to 'bear the contempt of his enemies, and the laughter of his friends, than undergo the pain of telling a story which might seem a panegyric upon himself' (I, 10, 24). He keeps quiet about what he is, in order to join others in mocking something that ought not to be the subject of laughter or condemnation. The awareness of the Fool purges the quixotic magnanimity of its madness, and the quixotic madness camouflages a noble-mindedness which, when manifested, would have to appear mad anyway.

As Fool, Yorick applies his consciousness to himself instead of to the world, while as Don Quixote he separates the world from himself instead of filling it with his projections. In both cases he takes on the reverse aspect of the traditional role, though this does not stop him from continuing to be both Fool and Don Quixote. He constantly separates himself from himself, in order to commune with himself as someone else. But communing with himself as someone else does not mean leaving himself. It is this extraordinary relationship within the self-splitting self that makes Yorick seem eccentric, in the sense of decentred. Mirroring oneself in another self and never allowing the other self to dominate the relationship, indicates to what extent such an activity has internalised the difference which otherwise exists between self and world. 'Positioned eccentrically, he stands where he stands, and at the same time not where he stands' (cf. Plessner, *Die Stufen des Organischen und der Mensch*, p. 342).

Maintaining this duality entails experiencing the self as suffering, but again there is nothing final about this suffering – it would disappear once the duality had been removed. It is true that Yorick dies 'quite brokenhearted' (I, 12, 31), but it is with a quotation from Sancho Panza on his lips 'and as he spoke it, Eugenius could perceive a stream of lambent fire lighted up for a moment in his eyes; – faint picture of those flashes of his spirit which (as Shakespeare said of his ancestor) were wont to set the table in a roar!' (I, 12, 32).

Turning tears to laughter makes Yorick's moment of parting both pathetic and comic. What appears to be a split in the personality constituted an ideal quality in the eighteenth century, as can be seen from the epitaph published fourteen years after Yorick's death in the novel, by the *Sentimental Magazine* (1774)

> He felt for man – nor dropt a fruitless tear,
> But kindly strove the drooping heart to chear . . .
>
> . . . with humour's necromantic charm,
> Death saw him sorrow, care, and spleen disarm.
>
> (see Tave, *The Amiable Humorist*, p. 190)

If Yorick was already the hero of Tristram's history, he now rises to the heights of a paradigm for the century. He combines two mutually exclusive frames of mind in a manner that would be impossible in real life. However, what is revealing here is less the reality than the conditions that give rise to it. The split in Yorick continually causes suffering to turn into laughter, ideals into foolery, and awareness into naïvety, but then the laughter, foolery and naïvety are themselves overturned because in dispatching their opposites they can only destabilise themselves. Through this constant overturning, it is impossible to reduce the self to an assumed core. Instead, everything springs from the split of the self, the basis of which remains unfathomable. Subjectivity thus appears in an unmistakable duality. It both fashions itself and exposes its self-production to failure. Hence *Tristram Shandy* presents subjectivity as pathological, a state evinced by its manic, melancholic and decentred manifestations. However, what can bring itself into being might also be able to cure itself. And so *Tristram Shandy* reveals subjectivity to be at one and the same time the pathological condition of the self and its cure. But if this applies to all subjectivity, there has to be particularisation to ensure that subjectivity remains individual. There are three modes of cure to be found in *Tristram Shandy*: mania is healed by play, melancholy by writing, and decentred eccentricity by suffering in silence. These modes depend on the individual nature of the split which fashions the subjectivity. Mania is unaware of the split, and so its manifestation is play. Melancholy feels it as difference between itself and what the self might be; and so writing constitutes the search for the knowledge withheld. Eccentricity highlights it as the division within itself; and so suffering in silence facilitates endurance of mutually exclusive frames of mind.

7   Wit and judgment

It follows that subjectivity cannot be deduced from anything pre-given; instead, it emerges in all its singularity from an oscillation set in motion by the various differences described, which need to be resolved. The force that guides this movement is *wit*, designed to link up what has been divided, and in so doing individualising subjectivity.

In the Author's Preface, Sterne embarks on a discussion of wit and judgment. The fact that he discusses wit here is evidence of its importance, and the fact that the Preface occurs only in Book 3 and not at the beginning sheds vivid light on the wit that has hitherto been practised. But if one is hoping to find out what wit actually is one will be disappointed, for the Preface merely pleads for wit and judgment to be given equal ranking, and suggests that a separation of the two is a '*Magna Charta* of stupidity' (*Author's Preface*, III, 163). This, of course, is a barb aimed at Locke, who had maintained

. . . that men who have a great deal of wit, and prompt memories, have not always the clearest judgment or deepest reason. For *wit* lying most in the assemblage of *ideas*, and putting those together with quickness and variety, wherein can be found any resemblance or congruity, thereby to make up pleasant pictures and agreeable visions in the fancy: *judgment*, on the contrary, lies quite on the other side, in separating carefully, one from another, *ideas* wherein can be found the least difference, thereby to avoid being misled by similitude, and by affinity to take one thing for another.   (II, 11, 2)

If wit serves the 'fancy', then the assemblage of ideas – which in turn springs from the need to bridge differences – must lose itself in the spontaneity of private impulses, in the freedom of improvisation, in the game of surprises – subject to whims that will dislocate all references. This is why the Shandys appear as 'fractured personalities' (Traugott (1954) p. 67), whose peculiarity runs chaotically through their lives. Yorick, too, meditating on the back of his ancient horse, points out 'that brisk trotting and slow argumentation, like wit and judgment, were two incompatible movements' (I, 10, 23). In this case, though, Locke would be right if the referential and unifying variety of wit and the analytical and separating operation of judgment moved off in different directions. But Yorick, even when he is dying, is still able to make people burst out laughing; therefore, why should he not be able to bring together that which Locke considered to be irreconcilable? In fact, the bridging of such a gulf allows combinations whose unpredictability makes the singularity of the self unmistakable. It is true that wit and judgment as incompatible movements follow different rhythms: the spontaneous devising of 'assemblages' is 'brisk' and the logical analysis of connections is slow; but in their respective functions each is equally indispensable, which is why Yorick on his steed 'could unite and reconcile everything' (I, 10, 23). Walter, however, draws his singularity almost exclusively from wit: 'proceeding from period to period, by metaphor and allusion, and striking the fancy as he went along (as men of wit and fancy do) with the entertainment and pleasantry of his pictures and images' (V, 6, 292).

It is not without significance that *Tristram Shandy* offers no definition of wit, even though it is very clearly upgraded. We have already noted that in the Author's Preface Tristram is only concerned with placing wit and judgment on a par, and towards the end of the novel we read that 'FANCY is capricious – WIT must be searched for' (IX, 12, 500). Traugott's definition may not be wrong, but is certainly inadequate: 'His statements in which the term "wit" is used show that he thought of wit as a way of communicating intuitive conceptions as opposed to the discursive determination of logic which is judgment' (Traugott (1954) p. 71). In so far as this definition is applicable, it would have meant that Sterne was merely expressing his views on a theme which preoccupied the eighteenth century but which could have nothing more than historical interest for us.

In *Tristram Shandy*, however, everything is two-sided. Defining wit would have required references; instead Sterne uses it in order to unfold the singularity of his characters, as wit allows for a spontaneous bridging of all possible differences. Its inventiveness is always individual, arising out of unforeseeable combinations to be derived from virtually every word and every gesture. Wit-inspired associations bracket the character's individuality with its unfathomableness, thus spotlighting its indefinable idiosyncrasy. Wit, therefore, serves the purpose of exploration, which here means that it enables the indefinable to be enacted.

Tristram's advocacy of the parity of wit and judgment now takes on a further dimension. As author of his life-story, he has both at his disposal in the balance he requires. His judgment enables him to use his wit for the incorporation of that which cannot be captured by judgment or by discourse. He uses wit to stage the singularity of his characters, and if he were to define it, he would lose the freedom to perform this enactment and would gain nothing in return. Furthermore, if wit as the driving force behind the exploration of subjectivity could be defined, then the basis of subjectivity would also become definable, in consequence of which its enactment would be superfluous, for staging is necessary only when what is to be presented is otherwise inaccessible. As Tristram gains this insight in the course of rendering his own life, he is anxious to exhibit that of others in terms of a stage-play, feigning to know the unknowable: 'my purpose is to do exact justice to every creature brought upon the stage of this dramatic work' (I, 10, 21). Through the play, the inaccessible basis of subjectivity is translated into the endless enactment of its singularity.

8 The discovery of communication by verbalising subjectivity

Since the characters in *Tristram Shandy* stand upon a stage, they are joined together by dialogue, and their singularity has to express itself through language. This process is a major theme in the novel, and once again it harks back to Locke. At first sight such recourse is plausible enough, for Locke frees language both from the realism of concepts and from the ternary relation of signs, and instead relates it to the activity of the human mind. 'I endeavour as much as I can to deliver myself from those fallacies which we are apt to put upon ourselves, by taking words for things' (II, 13, 18). Thus he argues against the realism of language, for '*words, in their primary or immediate signification, stand for nothing but the* ideas *in the mind of him that uses them*' (III, 2, 2). Words are not identical with things, but are merely signs of ideas for which there is no guaranteed linkage through any natural connection between sounds and concepts (for if there were, there would only be one language). The linkage occurs 'by a voluntary imposition whereby such a word is made arbitrarily the mark of such an *idea*' (III, 2, 1). The arbitrary connection between sign and idea disposes of the ternary relation of signs which – from Stoicism through to the Renaissance – saw signifier and signified tied to one another by a 'conjuncture'. The 'conjuncture', in turn, was the dominating pattern of the prevailing world pictures, which thereby imposed themselves on the use of language (cf. Foucault, *The Order of Things*, pp. 42ff.). In the binary relation of signs, the co-ordination of signified and signifier becomes arbitrary, one effect of which is to bring out the increased importance of the human mind, which now occupies the vacated position of the 'conjuncture'. Consequently language ceases to provide the grammar for prevailing world pictures, and even to be conceived as a copy of that world; instead it is free to perform a double function: '*First*, One for the recording of our own thoughts. *Secondly*, The other for the communication of our thoughts to others' (III, 9, 1).

This double function of language causes no difficulty for Locke, so long as it is a matter of articulating one's own ideas; the arbitrary nature of sign usage allows each individual to establish his own connection. Problems only arise when ideas are to be communicated, since the arbitrariness of sign relationships may lead to ideas that were not intended. Such sources of error are inherent in the inadequacy of words themselves, and in order to repair this deficiency, Locke proposes that one should define the names used to signify ideas, especially complex ones:

For since it is intended their names should stand for such collections of simple *ideas* as do really exist in things themselves, as well as for the complex *idea* in other men's minds which in their ordinary acceptation they stand for, therefore *to define their names right, natural history is to be inquired into*, and their properties are, with care and examination, to be found out.   (III, 11, 24)

Now this is precisely the recommendation followed by Walter Shandy, whose proliferating theories spring from the constant urge to define everything. There are critics who regard him as a realist concerning language, which would exile him from the Lockean camp, although in fact he is the most avid supporter of Locke in the whole Shandy family. Right from the start he is tormented by the denotative range of words. He

considers, for instance, what might have been the reasons that
led – during the phantom pregnancy of Mother Shandy – to
that fruitless journey to London:

. . . my father was out of all kind of patience at the vile trick and
imposition which he fancied my mother had put upon him in this
affair. – 'Certainly', he would say to himself, over and over again, 'the
woman could not be deceived herself; – if she could, – what weakness!'
– tormenting word! which led his imagination a thorny dance, and,
before all was over, played the deuce and all with him; – for sure as ever
the word *weakness* was uttered, and struck full upon his brain, – so sure
it set him upon running divisions upon how many kinds of weaknesses
there were; – that there was such a thing as weakness of the body, – as
well as weakness of the mind, – and then he would do nothing but
syllogize within himself for a stage or two together. How far the cause
of all these vexations might, or might not, have arisen out of himself.
(I, 16, 41)

As Walter talks to himself, there should not be any problems
of language here, for, as Locke observed,

for the recording of our own thoughts for the help of our own memories,
whereby, as it were, we talk to ourselves, any words will serve the turn.
For since sounds are voluntary and indifferent signs of any *ideas*, a
man may use what words he pleases to signify his own *ideas* to himself;
and there will be no imperfection in them if he constantly use the same
sign for the same *idea*, for then he cannot fail of having his meaning
understood; wherein consists the right use and perfection of language.
(III, 9, 2)

Although Walter Shandy associates a particular sign with a
particular idea, he finds that quite the opposite applies –
meaning is dispersed, and sets his imagination reeling. He
becomes a victim of Lockean measures of rectification, which
seek to ensure successful communication by eliminating 'the
imperfection of words' (III, 11, 1–23). Locke propounded a
two-tiered system of semiotics, consisting of the signifier and
the signified, and by means of definition he believed he could
achieve 'the proper *way to make known proper signification of
words*' (III, 11, 13). He even considered that morality could be
demonstrated *more geometrico*. But although his recognition of
language as a means of communication represented a
breakthrough, the abstract definition of signs was a step in the
wrong direction. Communication always occurs in situations,
and these can be such that one individual's fixed and inviolable

correspondence of signs and ideas will prevent any understanding with another individual. Walter therefore wonders whether he or something else is the cause of all his trouble; for him definition is the supreme regulator, and so the confusion in which he finds himself signalises that there is a situation that has been excluded from his conversation with himself. In Locke's terms, weakness is a specific name indicating a specific idea; but the signified meaning can only take on individuality when applied in a specific situation. As Walter wants to know the reason for Mother Shandy's weakness, his use of signs would have to be ternary (i.e. include the situation). Instead he clings to the binary concept, and so he cuts out the very situation to which the signs are meant to refer, so that now the situation – as it were ignored by the use of language – fights back against him and plunges his words into a kind of spin.

Such experiences serve to inflame still further Walter's passion for definition. Locke had maintained that the signification of one's own ideas would be infallible if the linguistic signs chosen for the purpose were used consistently. Thus it is virtually inevitable that Walter should become a theorist, since the consistency of theory allows him to ensure the correctness of his ideas. If in addition he is a rhetorician, this is to the extent that he has to put his certainty into operation in order to integrate all contradictions into his system. The result of this, however, is a continual rejection of realities, which have to be ignored in view of the indisputable validity of the premisses. Walter's theories are, therefore, concerned less with explanation than with exclusion, and what is excluded proceeds on more than one occasion to accumulate with catastrophic effects. Not only does Tristram receive the wrong name, but also his life leaves Walter's Tristrapaedia – meant to lay down the principles of education for his son – lagging behind, because the father's obsessive desire to regulate everything accelerates the speed with which the son's development escapes him. Instead of providing explanations, Walter's theories produce more and more gaps between themselves and their subject-matter, and the need to bridge these gaps simply increases the urge to produce theories. In this sense, the theories begin to backfire, for they produce the very thing that they are meant to eliminate.

Theory suppresses reality, though its declared intent is to grasp it, and so the pressure of reality itself makes more and more theories necessary. Having theories for everything entails a vast number of different theories which will have little in common with one another since they spring from different defensive requirements. The extent to which theory becomes all-encompassing can be seen from the fact that Walter equates his theories with reality, and in accordance with their multiplicity inhabits a multiplicity of realities. He is guided by an unconscious passion for removing the distinction between reality and its apprehension, but this results in an increase of distinctions, in so far as the more theories he forms, the more contradictions will arise between them. Since he lives for his theories, the contradictions lead to more theories, and these to more contradictions, and so on, with the result that difference becomes an ever more absurd keystone for his ideas. This is the reason for the giddy whirl into which he is plunged by the word 'weakness'. He is made to experience for himself the full force of difference, since the same word begins to mean different things for him. But in the face of Locke's assurances this should not be so, since language is supposed to function properly wherever its signs signify one's own ideas.

By isolating meaning from situation, Walter's use of language is doomed to failure, and his self-communication in danger of breaking down. In his refusal to recognise difference he becomes comic, especially since he is constantly confronted with it through his proliferating and contradictory theories. The comedy is both spontaneous and unambiguous, since it consists in the continual bombardment of theory by the realities that theory excludes, for nearly every theory brings about a misfortune which then needs to be neutralised by another theory.

This unnoticed and therefore comically stigmatised breakdown of Walter's self-understanding now in turn becomes a means of communication between text and reader, whose laughter indicates both awareness of the difference ignored and the need to inscribe difference into subjectivity in order for it to become conscious of itself. There is, however, an intriguing element in this comedy, which at first leads one to believe that like all comedy it contains a remedy, but then proceeds to break this promise, too. For the restitution of self-awareness to a self that is blind to reality constitutes less of a solution than a problem. Both Tristram and Yorick made this clear, for they possess what Walter lacks. If laughter is to be seen as the response to an evident defect, how is it that one continues to laugh at characters who have overcome that defect? The achievement of self-awareness is clearly not the answer to the problem of failed self-communication; but this very fact appears to render the seemingly fantastic nature of subjectivity all the more unfathomable.

There is a good deal of truth in Traugott's observation that Sterne 'was concerned almost exclusively with the problem of communication among men, and found enough fascination in merely exhibiting worldly phenomena for their rare instruction' (Traugott (1954) p. 72). The nature of this fascination can perhaps be gauged from the following example which is typical of conversations in *Tristram Shandy*. In the dialogue, the partner is an unavoidable reality so that the meaning of the utterance cannot be abstracted from the situation. It was Mother Shandy that brought about Walter's failure to communicate with himself, and in the following scene she is the point of reference for Walter and Toby's conversation:

Then it can be out of nothing in the whole world, quoth my uncle Toby, in the simplicity of his heart, – but MODESTY: – My sister, I dare say, added he, does not care to let a man come so near her††††. I will not say whether my uncle Toby had completed the sentence or not; – 'tis for his advantage to suppose he had, – as, I think, he could have added no ONE WORD which would have improved it. If, on the contrary, my uncle Toby had not fully arrived at his period's end, – then the world stands indebted to the sudden snapping of my father's tobacco pipe for one of the neatest examples of that ornamental figure in oratory which Rhetoricians style the *Aposiopesis*.

Just heaven! how does the *Poco più* and the *Poco meno* of the Italian artists, – the insensible MORE OR LESS, determine the precise line of beauty in the sentence, as well as in the statue! . . . O my countrymen! – be nice; – be cautious of your language; – and never, O! never let it be forgotten upon what small particles your eloquence and your fame depend.

– 'My sister, mayhap,' quoth my uncle Toby, 'does not choose to let a man come so near her††††.' Make this dash, – 'tis an Aposiopesis. – Take the dash away, and write *Backside*, – 'tis Bawdy. – Scratch Backside out, and put *Covered way* in, – 'tis a Metaphor; – and, I dare say, as fortification ran so much in my uncle Toby's head, that if he had been left to have added one word to the sentence, – that word was it.
(II, 6, 83f.)

As Tristram increases the variations possible for the completion of Toby's sentence, it becomes clear that language denotes not only situation but also attitude towards situation. While Locke believed that communication would succeed if all the speakers held to a precise definition of terms, Tristram accentuates the dual nature of words, which not only designate ideas but also the individuality of their usage. This implies that the meaning of words does not lie in their defined correspondence to ideas, but in their particular application. Locke's arbitrary link between sign and idea gives Sterne the chance to liberate words for their use, and application replaces definition as the reference for meaning. In this way, Sterne disclosed language as a problem of communication which for Locke was nothing but a purely mechanical transfer: 'To make words serviceable to the end of communication, it is necessary (as has been said) that they excite in the hearer exactly the same *idea* they stand for in the mind of the speaker' (III, 9, 6). Sterne, however, shows that communication is not a mechanical process. Words take on their special meaning according to the manner in which they are used, and precisely because they are common property, the speaker's subjectivity will be objectified through his own particular use. Thus *Covered way* means fortification to Toby, and something unseemly to Walter. Such incongruence reveals just how communication functions. This always entails interpretation by the hearer, and the implications of the utterance take on meaning in accordance with the dispositions of the partners, so that the attitude both of speaker and of hearer imprint themselves on what is said in the interchange, as can be inferred from the snapping of Walter's pipe. Communication, then, is not just a simple matter of transfer, but is a creative process whose product exceeds the contribution of each partner. Locke considered that definition would guarantee the correct transmission of ideas, but Sterne shows that successful communication is not possible through language alone. Historically speaking, language as a means of communication became a problematical issue at the moment when subjectivity moved into focus. Although subjectivity eludes language, it nevertheless determines the use of language. This elevates the question of reference to a paramount concern, and this can only be subjectivity itself, since any subjugation to a reference other than itself would move the self out of focus.

However, if subjectivity is to provide its own code, it follows that language will be used subjectively, too, and it is this that gives the Walter–Toby dialogue such a grotesque character.

The grotesqueness arises not so much from the misunderstand-
ings themselves as from the impression conveyed by them that
the compulsion to be precise makes subjectivity seem
phantasmal.

Clearly, then, communication in *Tristram Shandy* is a vehicle
for the representation of subjectivity. If language use reveals
subjectivity as a phantasm, it simultaneously indicates that
subjectivity defies verbalisation, in consequence of which
verbalised subjectivity manifests itself in a breakdown of
communication.

A vivid example of this is the conversation between Walter
and Toby, after the news of the death of Bobby – the heir to the
Shandy estate – appears to have deeply shaken the father.
Walter can only offer himself comfort by delving into his
classical treasure-chest of rhetoric. He quotes long passages
from a letter of condolence written by Servius Sulpicius, which
of course Toby does not know:

'Where is Troy and Mycenae, and Thebes and Delos, and Persepolis
and Agrigentum' – continued my father, taking up his book of post
roads, which he had laid down. – 'What is become, brother Toby, of
Nineveh and Babylon, of Cyzicus and Mitylene? The fairest towns that
ever the sun rose upon are now no more: the names only are left, and
those (for many of them are wrong spelt) are falling themselves by
piecemeals to decay, and in length of time will be forgotten, and
involved with everything in a perpetual night: the world itself, brother
Toby, must – must come to an end. 'Returning out of Asia, when I
sailed from Aegina towards Megara', (*when can this have been? thought
my uncle Toby*), 'I began to view the country round about. Aegina was
behind me, and Megara was before, Piraeus on the right hand, Corinth
on the left. – What flourishing towns now prostrate upon the earth!
Alas! alas! said I to myself, that man should disturb his soul for the loss
of a child, when so much as this lies awfully buried in his presence –
Remember, said I to myself again – remember thou art a man.' – Now
my uncle Toby knew not that this last paragraph was an extract of
Servius Sulpicius's consolatory letter to Tully. – He had as little skill,
honest man, in the fragments, as he had in the whole pieces of
antiquity. – And as my father, whilst he was connected in the Turkey
trade, had been three or four different times in the Levant, in one of
which he had stayed a whole year and a half at Zante, my uncle Toby
naturally concluded that in some of these periods he had taken a trip
across the Archipelago into Asia; and that all this sailing affair with
Aegina behind, and Megara before, and Piraeus on the right hand, etc.
etc., was nothing more than the true course of my father's voyage
and reflections. – . . . And pray, brother, quoth my uncle Toby, laying

the end of his pipe upon my father's hand in a kindly way of interruption – but waiting till he finished the account – what year of our Lord was this? – 'Twas no year of our Lord, replied my father. – That's impossible, cried my uncle Toby. – Simpleton! said my father, – 'twas forty years before Christ was born. My uncle Toby had but two things for it; either to suppose his brother to be the wandering Jew, or that his misfortunes had disordered his brain. – 'May the Lord God of heaven and earth protect him and restore him,' said my uncle Toby, praying silently for my father, and with tears in his eyes.   (V, 3, 288f.)

In contrast to previous dialogues between these two men, the breakdown of linguistic communication here has several causes. By quoting the consolatory letter, Walter appropriates it in order to give voice to his grief; but the fact that this is delivered in a comparatively well-defined situation, and that uncle Toby is actually spoken to, has an influence on the speech. It is abstracted from its immediate context (the death of Bobby) and yet the latter remains present because it has been invoked by Walter. Language therefore takes on a double meaning: that which Walter intends, and that which it receives through the context. Thus the separated context works back on the self-addressed speech, which then ceases to be the mere quotation of a consolatory letter and instead becomes the sign of an uncontrollable *double entendre*.

Walter's speech becomes equivocal in another respect, too. When he quotes the letter in order to soften the blow he has suffered from fate, he transfers Servius Sulpicius' words to his own situation. These, therefore, have the meanings a) of what they say, and b) of Walter's ideas. He has to hold fast to the literal meaning in order to give the right weight to the figurative, although at no time is he aware of this double usage. His unawareness is made all the more conspicuous by his observation on the wrong spelling of Greek names, where a difference between himself and what he reads becomes apparent and yet he still remains unconscious of it.

Toby, on the other hand, is a Lockean. He tries to associate words with corresponding ideas. For as he rightly assumes, language is perfect when it serves to reflect one's own ideas (cf. Locke III, 9, 2). This is why he recalls his brother's being in the Levant, so that he can understand what he hears by relating it to what he assumes to be Walter's ideas. But the result is that he can only grasp the figurative meaning as something literal, which inevitably flattens the two layers of meaning into one.

Toby thus performs the restorative operation on language recommended by Locke: he removes the distinction between figurative and literal meaning. The result, however, is a breakdown in communication.

The failure is exacerbated by the fact that Toby's use of language leads him to create a context of which he is just as unaware as Walter. The fact that at such a moment of grief Walter should be reporting on his business trips to the Levant naturally seems absurd to Toby. He has now created for the figurative signifiers a context that will enable him to understand what he considers to be Walter's literal meaning, if he assumes that his brother is mad. For he believes in the Lockean maxim that '. . . he should *use the same word constantly in the same sense*' (III, 11, 26). Walter, however, is not 'mad' for the reasons Toby supposes, but rather because his manic obsession suppresses the double meaning of language – although he of all people, as a rhetorician, should be aware of the different modes of language usage. Only the reader is aware of the difference, as he is made to perceive these modes by means of failed interchange.

The failure brings out Locke's nonsensical insistence on the strict separation of the literal from the figurative meaning. This could only be maintained so long as the situational context had no influence on the meaning. Sterne's view of this separation is almost emblematically encapsulated in the tale of the Abbess of Andouillet. Separating words along these lines deprives them of effect, as demonstrated by the abbess and the nun who try to get their mules moving by alternately calling *bou* and *ger*. The animals refuse to move, and the only person to understand the two women is the Devil (VIII, 25, 412) and – as far as the *double entendre* is concerned – presumably also the reader.

The dialogue shows that subjectivity comes to the fore through failures of communication, and thus it cannot be covered by language. In terms of language, therefore, communication fails; in terms of non-verbal gestures, there is at least a movement towards understanding.

Finally, the failure of language opens up a dimension which in *Tristram Shandy* typifies subjectivity: the wordlessness of intersubjectively comprehensible gestures. This is shown by the tears in Toby's eyes, of which Tristram goes on to say: 'My father placed the tears to a proper account' (V, 3, 289). There is still ambiguity in these tears, for they may relate to spontaneous

grief at Walter's supposed madness, or to sympathy at Bobby's
death, but in both cases they represent wordless sympathy, thus
at least eliminating the double meaning that characterised the
spoken word.

The various levels described reveal a recurring feature: the
failure of Locke's philosophy of language serves to show that
communication is a form of language usage; the failure of
linguistic communication uncovers the social nature of man;
and the phantasm of verbalised subjectivity draws attention to
gesture as a means of intersubjective understanding. Therefore,
if language fails, it is only a step towards a new discovery: a
semiotics of the body, which represents a final link between the
self and the world.

9   The body semiotics of subjectivity as discovery of man's natural morality

The novel is permeated with the physical gestures of its
characters as well as with gestures incorporated by the narrator
into his own language. The failure of linguistic communication
turns out to be less the catastrophe of an apparently self-
imprisoned subjectivity than an incentive for exploiting its
potential for intersubjectivity. What characterises all the physical gestures is the fact that they bring about immediate
understanding. This is true not only of Toby's tears, but also of
the actions of others such as Bridget and Trim. The latter has
understood the 'manual exercise' of the former long before she
has given voice to her meaning (IX, 28, 519). The same applies
to the manner in which Trim drops his hat in order to express
the experience of Bobby's death, and also to the detailed
description of Trim's posture as he recites the sermon (II, 17,
99f.).

Body language becomes the medium for successful communication, emphasising the social nature of man and his
natural morality, as evinced by Toby's tears, his sincere gaze,
and his injured expression before which even Walter's heart
melts (cf. IV, 2, 221). The fact that this morality of Toby's
cannot be translated into language, and is therefore conceivable
only through gestures, indicates that it is a natural component
of human nature, which has its ultimate connection with the
world through the body. Only the semiotics of the body can
show and confirm the naturalness of this morality.

This appears to be Sterne's response to the historical situation of the Enlightenment. Empiricism of the Lockean persuasion had freed morality from the constrictions of Christian moral law as well as from the decrees imposed by the absolute state on its subjects, and therefore the problem arose as to what foundation morality could have. Without the promises of religion and the political objectives of the absolutist state, it was now a matter of basing morality on man himself – a task that plagued the empirical tradition right through to the age of analytic philosophy. Eighteenth-century discussion, from its beginnings in the debating clubs of the coffee-houses to its apogee in Kant's categorical imperative (cf. Koselleck, *Kritik und Krise*, pp. 41–8), sought to develop a rational morality. But rationality – just like the moral law of religion and the decrees of the state – demanded that morality be capable of verbalisation, which caused problems for a reason-based morality tied to language as its vehicle of articulation. Locke had already sensed this problem, and so he had inserted in his *Essay* a whole 'book' on words, not least because 'moral words' caused him deep misgivings:

Hence it comes to pass that men's names of very compound *ideas*, such as for the most part are moral words, have seldom in two different men the same precise signification, since one man's complex *idea* seldom agrees with another's, and often differs from his own, from that which he had yesterday or will have tomorrow.   (III, 9, 6)

Once again Locke thought that he could solve the problem by means of definition. Since the type of morality developed in the course of the eighteenth century was – by Locke's own definition – inseparable from reason, it remained dependent on language. This dependence it shared with the morality of the commandments, not least because the dictates of reason also require verbalisation.

It is, therefore, significant that in *Tristram Shandy* the morality expressed by body language always shines forth most clearly when linguistic communication breaks down. If this breakdown supplies the backdrop for the emergence of morality, then the wordless presence of the latter signalises a shift in the conceptualisation of morality by dispensing with rationality as its base.

The anchorage of morality in the body would seem to undermine the reason-orientated principles of eighteenth-century ethics, but in fact it radicalises their mainspring, which was to 'naturalise' morality by grounding it in man himself. What is more natural than the body, which alone can express the naturalness of morality? The manifestation of morality by bodily signs indicates a correspondence between the two – relieving morality of any need for substantiation as to its naturalness. Consequently, instead of abstract references like commandment, reason, rationality and definition, Sterne takes morality to be action.

What Sterne is providing here is more than just an answer to the historical problem of eighteenth-century ethics, in spite of the fact that his conception of morality uncovered the displacements caused by rational ethics. By placing morality in a pre-language setting and expressing its naturalness through the body, he also attributes to idiosyncratic subjectivity a quality which endows it with its uniqueness – namely, a direct familiarity with itself. This familiarity explains nothing and cannot be grasped by the characters themselves, by other characters, or even by the narrator. It manifests itself through continual individualisations, when the characters use language, express opinions, and build up their own worlds, between which ever greater gulfs begin to yawn. This individualisation is a constant moving away from one another, and it would not be possible as an activity if each of the characters enclosed in the narrow confines of Shandy Hall did not possess that inaccessible but nonetheless obvious familiarity with the self. It is this familiarity with the self that gives the impetus for all their idiosyncratic behaviour. What subjectivity reveals of itself is like a continual staging of this familiarity, which remains silent as to its origin, just as none of its manifestations coincide with the latter. Yet this familiarity with itself would remain totally elusive, if it did not constantly translate itself into activities of individualisation, which may be re-enacting battles, writing a Tristrapaedia, etc. etc. – none of which, however, roots out what subjectivity is.

Subjectivity, then, may be viewed as a sort of differential that regulates the ever changing relations between the character's immediate familiarity with himself and the individualisations that result from this familiarity. It is out of this graded shifting that the unmistakable differences of the character emerge. But what all the characters have in common is precisely this familiarity with the self which – anterior to language and thought – has its foundation in the body, whose own language makes understanding possible. It is therefore not unreasonable in Sterne to equate such an understanding with morality, although it might also be argued that Sterne uses this body-language morality as a concept to illuminate the immediate familiarity of the self with itself.

This portrayal of subjectivity covers the historical response Sterne made to eighteenth-century rational morality by countering the latter with the non-verbalised wisdom of the body. Sterne's conception of morality, therefore, spells out both a historic situation and the constitutive conditions of subjectivity; this double function, exercised simultaneously, endows it with an aesthetic potential. For it renders conceivable that which language cannot capture, and which philosophic discourse was unable to substantiate: subjectivity is never finally defeated in spite of its self-imprisoning singularity. What cannot be explained can only be shown, and in 'showing' *Tristram Shandy* not only turned into a stage, but also into an outstanding eighteenth-century event whose impact is far from waning even today.

10   Eighteenth-century anthropology

Sterne's mode of rendering subjectivity is derived from another field of reference which might sweepingly be called eighteenth-century anthropology, and which cannot be as exactly pinpointed as Locke's empiricism. In the very first sentence of *Tristram Shandy* reference is made to the theory of the humours. The narrator fears that 'the fortunes of his whole house might take that turn from the humours and dispositions which were then uppermost' (I, 1, 9), and a little later we read of Yorick that

instead of that cold phlegm and exact regularity of sense and humours you would have looked for in one so extracted – he was, on the contrary, as mercurial and sublimated a composition . . . with as much life and whim . . . as the kindliest climate could have engendered and put together.   (I, 11, 27)

The theory of the humours was developed in Late Antiquity and flourished right through the end of the Middle Ages. With its four cardinal fluids, it was a physiological and therefore a natural definition of man, which in the sixteenth and seventeenth centuries served poets as the main store-house of patterns for representation of man, especially in relation to extreme or unbalanced modes of behaviour. The Elizabethans designated as *humourists* all authors whose subject-matter was the respective humours of others.

By the end of the seventeenth century the doctrine had been adapted to describe contemporary situations, in the course of which it became more and more historicised. For Sir William Temple, the humour was already a mannered form of behaviour, which – though one was born with it – had a conspicuous boom in England (Tave (1967), p. 98). From Congreve up until late in the eighteenth century, the climate was held responsible – and indeed Sterne regards Yorick's peculiarity as being conditioned by the weather. In addition to the climate, England's social conventions were regarded as feeding-grounds for the humour as a form of eccentricity – and indeed, eccentricity became the hallmark of humour. Thus humour was considered the offshoot of given social and meteorological conditions, leading to ever increasing individualisation for which 'eccentricity' turned out to be the common denominator (cf. Tave (1967) pp. 100–4).

This marked the virtual disappearance of humour as a particular constant in the human make-up, and it only remained present in the idea of the *ruling passions*, to which man was always succumbing and whose destructive effect was described by Pope in his *Essay on Man* (1733/4) as follows:

> Hence different passions more or less inflame,
> As strong or weak, the organs of the frame;
> And hence one master passion in the breast,
> Like Aaron's serpent, swallows up the rest.
>
> (Epistle II, 129–32)

Ruling passion and eccentricity are the terms which signify the change to which the inherited theory of the humours had been subjected by the eighteenth century. What was originally a physiological explanation of man has turned into peculiar features requiring correction – features which may bring man's nature into sharper focus (ruling passion), or may show his nature as being conditioned by his environment (eccentricity caused by the prevailing climate), and which stand in need of rectification if the effects are not to be damaging. For this reason the whole range of comedy, from satire to humour, is mobilised in order to cast human nature in its peculiar disfigurements, yet with the implicit promise that these can be rectified and its basic goodness will be left untouched. In

Tristram Shandy there are echoes of the humour's climatic conditioning and also of Pope's ruling passions: 'When a man gives himself up to the government of a ruling passion, – or, in other words, when his HOBBY-HORSE grows headstrong, – farewell cool reason and fair discretion!' (II, 5, 78).

The different strands which mark the reception of the theory of the humours in the eighteenth century have been gathered in the umbrella concept of the hobby-horse. It brackets together eccentricity and ruling passion, thereby removing the typically eighteenth-century distinction between dangerous and lovable obsession. Sterne shares the general view that a representation of human nature must fall back on the humour tradition as an accumulation of patterns if it is to be seen as itself and not as a bearer of meaning, but what concerns him is not the need for correction so much as the possible basics of human nature itself. Tristram believes that if we still possessed

Momus's glass in the human breast . . . nothing more would have been wanting, in order to have taken a man's character, but to have taken a chair and gone softly, as you would to a dioptrical beehive, and looked in, – viewed the soul stark naked; – observed all her motions, – her machinations; – traced all her maggots from their first engendering to their crawling forth; – watched her loose in her frisks, her gambols, her capriccios; and after some notice of her more solemn deportment, consequent upon such frisks, &c. – then taken your pen and ink and set down nothing but what you had seen, and could have sworn to: – But this is an advantage not to be had by the biographer in this planet.
                                                            (I, 23, 64)

What the Greek god Momus complained about to Hephaistos was the fact that men were not transparent, and this is the precondition for Tristram's representation of character. The fact that there are impenetrable hollows in human nature was neither viewed nor discussed in the various receptions which moulded the theory of the humours in the eighteenth century. Instead human nature, in order to attain self-perfection, had to be freed from all its past forms of subservience and become its own concern. Its very essence, so it seemed, had long been fixed by the interplay of the humours.

As he did with Locke, Sterne takes eighteenth-century anthropology and extracts what it ignored: the impermeable origin from which emerge ruling passions and eccentricity. If one accepts that human nature is not transparent, then all attempts at definition must be illusory. Therefore Tristram resolves: 'To avoid all and every one of these errors, in giving

you my uncle Toby's character, I am determined to draw it by
no mechanical help whatever; . . . I will draw my uncle Toby's
character from his HOBBY-HORSE' (I, 23, 65f.). But what
could be more mechanical than the old doctrine of the
humours, which saw human nature as an unbalanced mixture
of body fluids and believed that this explained man's nature,
even though the basis of the mixture remained unknown? Now
characterisation demands complete representation, which becomes problematical when character has ceased to be a bearer
of meaning. Whatever is visible can only point towards what
remains invisible. It is the latter, however, that has to be
fashioned, and this requires signs unmistakably marked as
being mere substitutes for what eludes capture, in order that the
peculiarities of the ungraspable may be adumbrated. The
hobby-horse offers almost ideal conditions for this sort of
equivalent. As regards its external shape, the 'stick [is] . . .
neither a sign signifying the concept horse nor is it a portrait of
an individual horse. By its capacity to serve as a "substitute"
the stick becomes a horse in its own right' (Gombrich,
*Meditations on a Hobby Horse and other Essays on the Theory of
Art*, p. 2). But if the stick is neither a reproduction of nor an
abstraction from something given, then it would seem to invite
ideas relating less to the image of a horse than to the function of
riding. As a 'substitute' the hobby-horse stands for an activity
which allows the re-enactment of what animates the rider.

This is the formal structure that Tristram has in mind when
he seeks to characterise Toby by way of his hobby-horse:

A man and his HOBBY-HORSE, though I cannot say that they act
and react exactly after the same manner in which the soul and body do
upon each other: Yet doubtless there is a communication between
them of some kind . . . By long journeys and much friction, it so
happens that the body of the rider is at length filled as full of HOBBY-
HORSICAL matter as it can hold; – so that if you are able to give but a
clear description of the nature of the one, you may form a pretty exact
notion of the genius and character of the other. Now the HOBBY-
HORSE which my uncle Toby always rode upon was, in my opinion,
an HOBBY-HORSE well worth giving a description of, if it was only
upon the score of his great singularity.   (I, 24, 66)

Now this implies that singularity can be brought to view in
relation to a difference by means of which Toby is split up into a
duality, thus allowing his nature to be mirrored by his hobby-
horse. The more successful the description of the hobby-horse,
the more tangible will be the genius and the character. This

strange duality does not correspond exactly to that of the soul and body, but the substitutional hobby-horse does refer to the 'genius', which always – both in its ancient and its pre-Romantic meaning – embodies a creative potential. The hobby-horse says something about this 'genius', and so has the effect of bringing it into view.

The relationship shows that human nature is not directly identical with the hobby-horse, as might have been suggested by eighteenth-century anthropology, which equated ruling passion, eccentricities, oddities, and whims with human nature. On the contrary, there is a lively interaction between 'genius/character' (as representatives of human nature) and the hobby-horse, with the latter reflecting nature, and the reflection in turn imprinting itself on the character. Through the hobby-horse, human nature takes on a tangible form, which it needs if it is to become active, and during this process it increasingly resembles the reflection of itself cast by the mirror. The hobby-horse does reveal a certain social conditioning which results from the character's situation in the world, but it never loses its status as an imaginary manifestation of human nature.

This mirroring is necessary since subjectivity is what it is by being self-related. The hobby-horse is therefore a substitute in two senses. First, it replaces all those functions which had made the character into the bearer of meaning other than itself. Secondly, it enables human nature to unfold itself in the world on its own conditions. This turns the hobby-horse into a sign for liberating the self from all subservience, as well as for indicating that the self can only take full possession of itself by way of imagining itself. As a replacement for all the character's subjugation in narrative literature, the hobby-horse at one and the same time is a schema brought forth by the 'genius' and also allows the 'genius' – by representing its ungraspability – to give itself palpable substance.

This dialectical play traces the outline of the characters, which diverge from one another whether or not they are aware of this strange doubling of themselves. For the fact that there is a split running through subjectivity is known to Tristram, but not to Toby and not even to Walter, the great know-all himself. Indeed Tristram's awareness of it is essential if subjectivity is to be demonstrated through the hobby-horse as a double of human nature. Without such a doubling, subjectivity as itself would be impossible to capture, and for Walter and Toby it does remain a closed area, as they are unable to assume an attitude towards their hobby-horses.

The more the hobby-horse coincides or even fuses with the 'genius' – although as the imaginary mirror it is meant only to bring it to the fore – the more phantasmal it becomes. The phantasm indicates that the distinction between '[a] man and his HOBBY-HORSE' has been eliminated, thus making subjectivity congeal into the bizarre form of its self-image. To turn the mirror into a reality in its own right entails *en*closing the self through that which was meant to *dis*close subjectivity. As a phantasm the hobby-horse reflects the ruinous self-distortion of subjectivity by its own fantasy – a fantasy which also offers the self the opportunity to view itself by means of doubling. The hobby-horse is therefore identical neither with ruling passions, nor with eccentricities, but instead it represents the duplicity of fantasy.

In the second half of the eighteenth century, the hobby-horse was an apt means of elucidating this duplicity in that – as Ian Watt rightly points out – it did not yet have the 'modern approbative sense', but was regarded, rather, as 'an imitation horse, such as was used in the mummers' dance or as a child's toy; so a concern with hobbyhorses in an adult had, to an earlier generation, seemed a frivolous derogation of man's stature as a rational animal' (Watt, 'The Comic Syntax of *Tristram Shandy*', p. 326). Even if reason is not to be denied to subjectivity, nevertheless Sterne did not equate it with subjectivity, which would lose its oddity and whimsicality if reason were its governing force. Instead, subjectivity grasps itself in the reflection of itself, and the latter need not necessarily be its rationality. If the hobby-horse, then, appears to be a 'frivolous derogation', this is mainly because the imaginary manifestation so overwhelms the characters that they coincide with their own fabrications. As the characters are not aware of this dialectical play, they have to be plunged into comedy, in order at least to alert the reader to what they are constantly glossing over. It is not surprising, therefore, that Tristram uses block capitals whenever he talks of hobby-horses. This graphic distinction draws attention to the multiple functions of the hobby-horse.

As a phantasm it fills the hollow space from which subjectivity emerges; consequently it congeals into an oddity which delineates the singularity of the self. Indeed, as frozen fantasy this phantasm conveys an experience of singularity whose bizarre manifestation proves to be resistant to interpretation.

The latent comedy of the hobby-horse draws attention to the fact that subjectivity is a relationship of the self to itself, and consequently cannot be identical with the peculiarities of its individual manifestations. Comedy stresses the possibility of correcting the distortions it exposes. But as a self-related subjectivity cannot be grasped through extraneous references, it can only reflect on the dialectical play from which it has emerged, so that the comedy of the hobby-horse actually signalises obliviousness to the necessity for this self-reflection.

A further function of the hobby-horse is to act as a bridge to the reader. It makes the intangible conceivable by showing that the imponderable depths of subjectivity can only be illuminated by way of imagery. The hobby-horse stimulates the reader's imagination, '[as] it compels us to refer every figure and every object shown to that imaginary reality which is "meant"' (Gombrich (1965) p. 10). As an imaginary means of access to the reality of subjectivity, the hobby-horse parades itself in a whole range of forms by way of latent comedy, which leaves no doubt as to the substitutional nature of the beast. Therefore Tristram spotlights the relation between 'genius' and 'HOBBY-HORSE', so that the reader can never take the appearance for reality. And yet precisely for this reason, there arises the necessary degree of tension to make the reader follow the trail of what is concealed rather than what is revealed by the rich offerings of conceivable realities. This highlights the ineradicable dual significance of the hobby-horse: its substitutional aspect signalises the inaccessibility, and its schematic aspect the conceivability of subjectivity. And so the hobby-horse finally ceases to be a mere name for ruling passions or eccentricities conditioned by climate or society, as was the case in the eighteenth-century reception of the theory of the humours. Now Sterne transforms this principal component of eighteenth-century anthropology into a metaphor for the perceptibility of subjectivity – a subjectivity which he had uncovered as the hidden referential instance of Locke's theory of cognition, and which he had brought into view by overturning that theory.

Chapter II

Writing strategies

1 The first-person narrator

Shall we forever make new books, as apothecaries make new mixtures, by pouring only out of one vessel into another? Are we forever to be twisting and untwisting the same rope? forever in the same track – forever at the same pace? Shall we be destined to the days of eternity, on holy days as well as working days, to be showing the *relics of learning*, as monks do the relics of their saints – without working one – one single miracle with them? (V, 1, 279)

Writing poses the question of how to relate to traditions of writing, and this would seem to entail nothing other than a continual reclassification of that which already exists. Tristram, however, wants writing to consist in rewriting the written, as he demonstrates above by reworking a passage in Robert Burton's *Anatomy of Melancholy*:

As apothecaries, we make new mixtures every day, pour out of one vessel into another; and as those old Romans robbed all the cities of the world, to set out their bad-sited Rome, we skim off the cream of other men's wits, pick the choice flowers of their tilled gardens to set out our own sterile plots . . . we weave the same web still, twist the same rope again and again. (Burton, *The Anatomy of Melancholy*, pp. 23f.)

The Burton text shines like a palimpsest through Tristram's complaint. Instead of the old matter being constantly poured from one vessel into another, tradition ought to be taken as the material from which miracles are to be wrought. By 'plagiarising' the Burton text, Sterne brings out that which the latter did not say, and thus he articulates an essential mode relating to tradition. For every tradition produces a silence by what it says, and traditions perpetuate themselves through the sequent articulation of what has remained unsaid. These unavoidable omissions open up a space for interpretation, which is necessary for the subsequent appropriation of the tradition, whose features are bound to change if its impact is to be preserved within the new context. If the inherited silence, however, is to be exploited in such a way that its interpretation is like a miracle, then the tradition will not be obliterated but relegated into the background against which the miracle can be conceived for what it is. This is what happens to the narrative tradition in *Tristram Shandy*.

It must first be said that in view of the subject-matter unfolded in *Tristram Shandy*, an omniscient narrator is out of the question, for this would be in direct conflict with the unfathomableness of subjectivity. He who knows everything is obviously incapable of not knowing, and thus incapable of conveying the limitations of knowledge as a means of experiencing subjectivity. To communicate this 'message' the gnostic narrator would either have to narrate the demise of his own knowledge, or to transform unfathomable subjectivity into a sign for something else.

Sterne therefore needed a self-related narrator who would be of the same stamp as the other subjective selves which he is trying to understand. From the plethora of narrative techniques, that of the first-person narrator was clearly the most apposite, for he is a character among characters, and is therefore involved in the events he describes. This form, however, as practised in the eighteenth century, was frequently no more than a disguise for the authorial perspective, since the ordinary first-person narrator had survived all the dangers, and was thus orientated by hindsight which gave him a detached and panoramic view of his life virtually no different from that of the omniscient narrator.

The eighteenth-century tradition remained silent about the question of what it is to be caught up in the midst of things without having recourse to a grand-stand view that would facilitate an answer. Indeed, first-person narration as practised in the eighteenth century completely bypassed this 'being in the midst', which was at best only one stage along the road to the culmination of the life story and was therefore shaped in accordance with the meaning that emerged from the end. Sterne, however, takes the first-person view at face value by articulating precisely what had hitherto been ignored, namely the immediacy of experience before it has been coloured by the knowledge of what it may serve. Thus Tristram can proclaim that 'write as I will, and rush as I may into the middle of things, as Horace advises, – I shall never overtake myself' (IV, 13, 231).

It is this inability to overtake himself in his writing that enables him to stay in and to communicate 'the middle of things', so that writing itself produces the elusiveness of the object being written about. Indeed writing cannot do anything but chase in vain, and the faster the writer rushes after his own life, the faster it will move to avoid his grasp. It is like trying to catch one's own shadow. Tristram is fully aware of all this:

I am this month one whole year older than I was this time twelvemonth; and having got, as you perceive, almost into the middle of my fourth volume – and no farther than to my first day's life – 'tis demonstrative that I have three hundred and sixty-four days more life to write just now, than when I first set out; so that instead of advancing, as a common writer, in my work with what I have been doing at it – on the contrary, I am just thrown so many volumes back . . . I should just live 364 times faster than I should write – It must follow, an' please your Worships, that the more I write, the more I shall have to write.
(IV, 13, 230f.)

This statement will only appear paradoxical to those who believe that the first-person narrative is a reproduction of life and not – as in fact it is – an illusion necessary in order to endow a pre-set meaning with the essential degree of probability (an attempt, incidentally, that underlies all realistic narratives). Tristram wants to write his life-story, which can only remain in view if he deliberately distorts the inherited narrative convention, in order that experience of being in 'the midst of things' may be communicated.

Speculation as to whether *Tristram Shandy* is a fragment or not is therefore pointless; being in the midst can only be ended by death, and not by any all-embracing meaning. This is not to say that being in the midst of things is meaningless – on the contrary, it produces many more significances than can be revealed by any teleologically-orientated story. But this multiplicity of significances is only possible because of their disconnectedness, their varied range and direction, and – last but not least – the conflicts between them, all of which together converge into a topography of life.

Furthermore the first-person narrative offers latitude to bring out other aspects of what it means to be plunged into the midst of things. Structurally this narrative scheme has alternated between an experiencing and a reflecting self, thus demonstrating how experience is to be processed into meaning. No matter how diverse the intention might have been, the practice from *Robinson Crusoe* right through to Smollett's picaresque variants had always been for the narrator – despite all the mishaps he encountered on the way – finally to reach the goal originally mapped out for him. In this traditional usage, the pattern entailed initial disjunction between self and world, which gave rise to the development of objectives whose realisation eliminated the disjunction.

It is the absence of any such ultimate meaning that results in the predominance of the disjunction, so that the traditional self-fulfilment of the first-person narrator can never take place in *Tristram Shandy*. Tristram therefore has to chase after his own life, and furthermore must confess: 'I begin with writing the first sentence – and trusting to Almighty God for the second' (VIII, 2, 438). The gulf between 'I' and the world cannot be bridged by any given premiss, but instead has to be explored; for this purpose the storehouse of traditions can supply nothing more than instruments. For Tristram, it must be said again, brings out that which tradition has been silent about, and yet it is precisely his relation to that tradition which enables him to articulate what had remained unsaid. He now explores the gulf between self and world which has been glossed over – for whatever reason – in the traditional first-person form, but in order to do so he must renounce something that had hitherto been taken for granted as a basic element of that form: narration. Exploring can only take place if the objective of exploration is always present, whereas narration depicts a 'mythical analogue' (cf. Lugowski, *Die Form der Individualität im Roman*, pp. 52ff.) – something preordained which can only become tangible by way of a narrated story. By contrast, the episodes of Tristram's life are so bare of overarching references that they obliterate any form of mediation between self and world, thereby exemplifying an essentially unconditioned approach to the narrator's life. In writing, therefore, Tristram must guard against narration so that the gulf which he wishes to explore will not be covered over by the connecting weave of a story. His writing must be a record only of his discoveries. Therefore Tristram must take heed never to become a successful historian of his life (cf. Warning (1965) pp. 15–24). Success would lift him out of the midst of things, allowing him to adopt a stance outside them which would mean representing not life itself, but what had become of it.

Since he must not tell the story of his life, Tristram has to seek

success elsewhere. What is left to orientate him if in his search
he has to beware of narration? Traditional premises are no
help to him, and so in his affliction he cries out:

Blessed Jupiter! and blessed every other heathen god and goddess! for
now ye will all come into play again, and with Priapus at your tails –
what jovial times! – but where am I? and into what a delicious riot of
things am I rushing? I – I who must be cut short in the midst of my
days, and taste no more of 'em than what I borrow from my
imagination.   (VII, 14, 400)

Becoming one's own last refuge means that one can only have
recourse to one's own imagination. And this, of course, makes
the first-person narrator's mode of writing highly subjective,
which has caused many critics to call the book chaotic. E.M.
Forster's remark may be taken as typical: 'Obviously a god is
hidden in *Tristram Shandy*, his name is Muddle' (Forster (1958)
p. 105). But those who consider the novel to be a jumble should
bear in mind the fact that Tristram himself has already
anticipated the description – though his comment has a certain
sting in the tail: 'I write a careless kind of civil, nonsensical,
good-humoured Shandean book, which will do all your hearts
good – – And all your heads too, – provided you understand it'
(VI, 17, 356). What is it that has not been understood by those
who think the novel is nothing but the unbridled meanderings
of the imagination?

Perhaps the first thing is the distance between Tristram's
imagination and that which his imagination grasps. His
awareness of this gap prevents his last refuge from becoming a
mere phantasm, such as afflicts all those who are ignorant of the
ineradicable difference between imagination and reality. Tristram exposes his own fantasy himself, in order to show that what
it has grasped is an imposed pattern, and also to show that
being in the midst of life requires such patterns to give form to
its ungraspability. But these forms must not – as narratives
usually do – represent life or pass themselves off as constituents
of life; instead they must be revealed as necessary, pragmatic
interventions. Only in this way can it be made clear beyond
doubt that they are nothing but instruments, which explains
both their plurality and their contradictoriness. In view of the
fact that they are still forms of narrative, the narrator is bound
to draw attention to the difference between the approach and
the life approached, which requires incessant reflection on his

own writing. Not only does this enable him to keep open the gap between self and world – a gap which traditional first-person narratives always aimed to close – but it also shows that the gulf is to be explored by deconstructing narration itself.

Thus, strange as it may seem, it is only a subjective mode of writing that can convey an impression of the elusiveness of life when written about – not least because an objective elusiveness would presuppose a knowledge that in turn would deprive writing of its purpose. But if writing is an exploration of something withheld from us – i.e. what one's own life actually is – then imagination turns out to be the last resort, whose images, however, should bear the mark of contrivance, for otherwise they might be taken for the goal itself instead of pointers to the goal.

Tristram must therefore write against narration, whose exemplariness always indicates that it stands for something else. All narrative is basically metaphorical, whereas Tristram's writing is metonymical, and in order to highlight this substitution, Sterne reinforces his narrator's metonymy with irony, making the distinctions unmistakable. Such a mode of writing demands strategies which run almost diametrically counter to the narrative tradition of the eighteenth century, because they must incorporate the unbridgeable distance which separates them from life. The strategies developed to this end by the first-person narrator are those of interruption, digression and equivocation.

2   Interruption

Writing, when properly managed (as you may be sure I think mine is), is but a different name for conversation: As no one who knows what he is about in good company would venture to talk all; – so no author who understands the just boundaries of decorum and good breeding would presume to think all: The truest respect which you can pay to the reader's understanding is to halve this matter amicably, and leave him something to imagine, in his turn, as well as yourself.   (II, 11, 90)

It is characteristic of conversation that one can never know precisely what will emerge from it (cf. Gadamer, *Wahrheit und Methode*, p. 361). This is due not only to the different standpoints of the participants, but also – and rather more significantly – to the need to interpret statements through their implications. 'In authentic conversation, then, one listens not only to what is said but to the unsaid, the horizon of meaningfulness, that wells up within it' (Swearingen, *Reflexivity in Tristram Shandy*, p. 13). Thus, if a conversation is to be successful, the partners will have to reach beyond what is familiar to them, and grasp something that had hitherto not lain within their 'horizon'. This process, according to Tristram, demands an effort on both sides, since the conversation is not only conducted by the partners, but the partners are also conducted by the conversation. And since he regards writing as conversation, it follows that he cannot know in advance where he is going.

Writing, then, is speech, and its task is to transcribe the voices which talk to one another. It has to renounce itself in order to articulate speech, which makes writing explode into plurivocity. Even when Tristram appears to be speaking alone, more often than not different voices seem to be interacting. The death-scene of Le Fever is a case in point:

The blood and spirits of Le Fever, which were waxing cold and slow within him, and were retreating to their last citadel, the heart – rallied back, – the film forsook his eyes for a moment, – he looked up wishfully in my uncle Toby's face, – then cast a look upon his boy, – and that *ligament*, fine as it was, – was never broken. – Nature instantly ebbed again, – the film returned to its place, – the pulse fluttered – stopped – went on – throbbed – stopped again – moved – stopped – shall I go on? – No.   (VI, 10, 347)

Dashes in *Tristram Shandy* are favoured marks for transcribing the voice. Their profusion here indicates agitated talk of something inevitable, which would lose its immediacy if it were merely to be narrated. And precisely because talk, unlike narrative, need pay no dues to syntax, it is able to convey spontaneity. The typographical signs that permeate Tristram's writing help to endow it with the quality of speech.

But who is speaking? Should it be Tristram, who was not even present at the scene he describes, although the closing question makes it clear that he *is* the one speaking? Does Tristram really see the death-throes as a retreat to the citadel, where the last resistance is to be organised? The military metaphor, and the intimate knowledge of Le Fever's death, would seem to imply an echo of Toby's voice as well as the presence of the author, who once confessed of *Tristram Shandy*: ''tis . . . a picture of myself' (*Letters of Laurence Sterne*, p. 87).

It would seem that Tristram's voice intertwines with others, and indeed the voice would be unrecognisable as his if he did not end the passage, and Le Fever's story, with the first-person question, which acts as a curtailment, conveying the inexpressible grief of Toby as well as the unspeakable sentimentality of the author. Writing as conversation must allow the reader to imagine what is meant, and for this purpose what is said can only be a guideline.

Tristram's voice is what holds everything together.

Through it Sterne discovered a principle of order which resides not so much in linear development in time as in a kind of timeless consistency of texture; it is this which has primary autonomy, and which controls every narrative element, from the phrase to the paragraph, the chapter, and the book.   (Watt (1967) p. 330)

Plurivocity here means that Tristram's speech unfolds as a continual dialogue with the characters, the author, and even with the reader, and thus the writing can never (and must never) become narration. Just as Tristram's voice is the bearer of other voices, his writing must always be the bearer of speech, for which the profusion of typographical marks remains an unmistakable sign. This applies particularly to the dash, which indicates the pauses, as well as the dialogue, changes of direction in thought, and also relative freedom from the logical constraints of grammar. It marks the openness of speech, which can branch off unexpectedly, go forwards or backwards, turn to the other characters or to the reader, and generally allow the flexibility necessary for conversation as the process of exploration. Syntactically the dash is an interruption, but as such it permits new links, thereby granting access to new territories.

The other typographical marks have a similar function. The many omissions, denoted by asterisks, invite the reader to complete the text himself, and also act as interruptions even when the exact number of missing letters is shown, enabling the reader to fill in the blanks. For what matters here is not the completion of indecent sentences (e.g. V, 17, 307) so much as creating a more intimate relationship between the narrator and the reader. The omissions are interruptions in the sense that they signal a change of level, from the matter under discussion to dialogue with the reader who, more often than not, is instigated to view the matter differently and bear the responsibility of what might issue from it.

It seems that the reader has to be equipped for such a dialogue. Thus, he is confronted with pages that are black, or mottled, or blank, and is constantly being jerked to attention by a pointing finger, and inversions or omissions of whole chapters so that he can always be present to himself in the condition of his own activated imagination. For he is to be drawn into a dialogue in which the narrator, the author and the characters are already mixed, if not mixed up. The reader's participation, however, must be such that he will be prevented from removing the plurivocity by means of his own projections. The narrator has been at pains to produce openness through his interruptions, and so it is essential that the reader should not be allowed to impose his own patterns, thereby closing up what has been opened. The best way to counteract this is to create a dialogic relationship between the reader and his own expectations, for it is recommended that in reading 'the mind should be accustomed to make wise reflections, and draw curious conclusions as it goes along' (I, 20, 52). And in order that these should not fall into already established patterns, we learn at the end of the very first book:

. . . inasmuch as I set no small store by myself upon this very account, that my reader has never yet been able to guess at anything. And in this, Sir, I am of so nice and singular a humour that if I thought you was able to form the least judgment or probable conjecture to yourself of what was to come in the next page, – I would tear it out of my book.

(I, 25, 68)

It is the reader's task to draw conclusions, but these must not be guided by his habitual expectations. He must distrust his habitual expectations if he is to realise that the said is merely a pointer to the implications. Instead of his expectations, it is his imagination that is to direct his comprehension, for only his imagination will enable him to follow the conversation of Tristram, 'who is a genius of implication' (Lehman, 'Of time, personality and the author', p. 33). Nothing is set out before the reader in the manner, for instance, of Fielding's 'bill of fare' at the start of *Tom Jones* (I, 1, 1), for there is no intention of establishing the common ground between text and reader that was so essential in other eighteenth-century novels. This new 'genre', with no antecedent support from tradition, requires the cooperation of the reader (cf. Lange, 'Erzählformen im Roman des achtzehnten Jahrhunderts', pp. 488f.), and the best way to obtain this is to manoeuvre the reader straightaway into the latent role of author, for in this way he will have to assume responsibility for everything himself. (For details see Preston, *The Created Self. The Reader's Role in Eighteenth-Century Fiction*, pp. 133–95.) Such a role entails the reader imagining whatever has been left out by the strategy of interruption.

What are the intentions and the organisation underlying this strategy? In order to answer this question, let us look at a single – though very lengthy – sentence:

I would sooner undertake to explain the hardest problem in Geometry than pretend to account for it that a gentleman of my father's great good sense, – knowing, as the reader must have observed him, and curious too in philosophy, – wise also in political reasoning, – and in polemical (as he will find) no way ignorant, – could be capable of entertaining a notion in his head so out of the common track, – that I fear the reader, when I come to mention it to him, if he is the least of a choleric temper, will immediately throw the book by; if mercurial, he will laugh most heartily at it; – and if he is of a grave and saturnine cast, he will, at first sight, absolutely condemn as fanciful and extravagant; and that was in respect to the choice and imposition of Christian names, on which he thought a great deal more depended than what superficial minds were capable of conceiving.   (I, 19, 47)

The issue here is Walter's linguistic realism, but instead of saying that for him the name and the object were identical, Tristram refracts the concept into a variety of colours. If writing is considered to be conversation, one cannot be sure from the start that what is being talked about is real or is leading anywhere, and in this respect the sentence epitomises Tristram's conversational mode of writing. The state of affairs is interrupted by the parentheses as well as by the invocation of different types of reader, but the proviso is that the shifting aspects will bring to light the inaccessibility of the matter under discussion.

In the narrator's parentheses Walter's obsession is refracted in the light of highly commendable qualities; the reactions that are called forth in the reader, however, bear the stamp of the humours, whose one-sidedness is basically no different from Walter's obsession. This similarity is pointed up by the fact that various judgments are attributed to different readers at a stage in the sentence where no one can possibly know what is to be judged. In view of his father's 'great good sense' and other abilities, it seems increasingly inexplicable to Tristram that his father should equate name with character (he goes on to say that his father believed 'there was a strange kind of magic bias, which good or bad names . . . irresistibly impressed upon our characters and conduct' I, 19, 47), and yet this same equation seems quite unproblematical when it concerns dismissal of the notion on the part of the different types of reader – but perhaps this is precisely because the readers are like Walter in that they concur unquestioningly with their own opinions. By way of that which astounds the narrator, the reader caricatures himself in his own certainty. The comedy reveals that this certainty is paid for by exclusion, and what is excluded is the reason for Walter's hobby-horse, the unfathomableness of which has been left in no doubt by the narrator.

What we have here, then, is a situation viewed from various standpoints, all of which aim at disclosure and none of which strike home. Consequently, the various judgments are nothing more than restricted perspectives which reflect the disposition of the viewer and not the nature of the object viewed.

Tristram's identification of his fictitious readers with various humours is certainly not unintentional. It shows the extent to which interpretations spring from dispositions that reveal more of the peculiarity of the observer than of the thing observed, which in fact they are meant to represent. For such an impression to be conveyed, however, forms of representation are necessary, and so the little assortment of humours offers a rapid shift of perspectives which fragment rather than represent the topic – Walter's equation of language with reality. Each perspective gives a different shape to something the narrator finds inexplicable, and therefore none of them can represent the state of affairs itself, but each represents nothing other than the respective humour. As a result, though, the different perspectives taken together transcend their own limitations in so far as their rapid shift, with no point of convergence, corresponds to the inexplicability of which the narrator himself is conscious. However inexplicable Walter's obsession might be, there can be no doubting its existence. It demands attitudes, forms of comprehension, of judgment, to translate the reality into the temperaments of those who look on it. And so Tristram's writing must be organised as conversation, because only this plurivocity can reveal the ever changing attitudes which, as refractions of what is, make reality conceivable as something happening. The individual voices – whether they belong to the characters or to the narrator, the author or the reader – are all strangely doubled, for they attempt to define reality, but in so doing they echo themselves. With the exception of Yorick, none of the voices evinces any awareness of this doubling. It is Tristram's task to make the reader aware of it, and so he is always careful not to give any set form to ungraspable realities. On the contrary, he must use the participants in his conversation to bring forth the double references of which they are unaware and from which reality may emerge as a process of realisation.

Many of the central episodes of the novel are structured in accordance with this pattern. A typical example is Trim's reading of Yorick's sermon on good conscience. The episode even begins with an interruption, for Walter 'as he opened his mouth to begin the next sentence' (II, 14, 98) never actually gets to speak it. Trim suddenly pops in to bring Toby his *Stevinus*, which at this juncture had already passed out of Toby's mind, but from it falls Yorick's sermon, the reading of which now gives rise to a whole series of interruptions.

Each character reacts to the sermon according to his own singularity. Trim adopts a theatrical pose corresponding to the dignity of his task, and he sheds copious tears over the death of his brother when the conversation turns to the Inquisition. Walter theorises about the authorship and the rhetorical rules of recitation; Toby tries to straighten out the military metaphors, and Dr Slop's reaction to the Protestant ethic of conscience is to fall asleep. Not one of them is concerned with the actual subject of the sermon, and their consciences are neither examined nor sharpened. Instead, there emerges once more what J. Paul Hunter calls 'the general motif in *Tristram Shandy* of watching the responder at work' (Hunter, 'Response as Reformation: *Tristram Shandy* and the art of interruption', p. 180). Here we see just how the human mind works. Regardless of the personal eccentricities of these particular characters, the process is always one of using our own projections to link up with the reality that confronts us. By caricaturing assumed readers, Sterne makes his real reader observe that realities – as in the case of the sermon – arise out of denaturing an occurrence, or – as in the case of Walter's notion of language – out of defining the indefinable. Whatever the initial impulse, reality is not something given but can only become present by way of realisation.

As far as the eighteenth-century novel was concerned, such an insight meant a radical change of perspective, for represented reality had hitherto served as the testing-ground for the hero, whose course of life determined to what extent reality actually was represented. This pattern, which the novel inherited from Puritan devotional literature, was to dominate its structure right through to the late nineteenth century, though with the difference that the world represented was no longer one of the hero's proving himself but of suffering.

Sterne's undermining of the conventional structures of represented reality is given added impetus by a story in which the strategy of interruption is intensified to the *nth* degree. This is the story of the King of Bohemia and his seven castles, which at Toby's request (VIII, 19, 454) Trim begins to 'narrate', although at best he can only 'narrate' the manner in which he is prevented from narrating it, for hardly has he begun the first sentence when Toby interrupts, so that he then has to begin all over again. The last in a whole series of interruptions brings out very strongly the reason why this story – like any other about life – cannot be told at all. Trim starts his story for the last time:

Now the King of Bohemia with his queen and courtiers *happening* one fine summer's evening to walk out – Aye! there the word *happening* is right, Trim, cried my uncle Toby; for the King of Bohemia and his queen might have walked out, or let it alone; – 'twas a matter of contingency, which might happen, or not, just as chance ordered it.
(VIII, 19, 461)

And from this point on, there is no further mention of the story of the King of Bohemia. As life 'happens', it resists representation by a story, for contingency cannot be narrated. But this fact itself requires a mode of representation, which turns out to be depicting 'happenings' through the impossibility of story-telling.

This example is typical of Sterne's writing. The strategy of interruption signalises the presence of life, in so far as whatever context is built up by the writing must be punctured in order that it should not be taken for life itself. Writing has to deconstruct itself so that whatever is being written about will be seen as something other than what is written. The interruptions are not, therefore, imitations of the contingency of life, for they are not related to life but to writing, which they break up into a discontinuous sequence of aspects. These, as they accumulate, show the degree to which life overshoots its aspects, each of which was intended to encompass it. This overshooting is a dynamic process which eludes capture through imagery, and yet is made conceivable through self-interrupting writing. By inscribing life into the writing through interruptions, Sterne is able to represent life as a happening.

For this to be possible, the narrator must not adopt any specific standpoint, for if he does, the happening will shrink to the dimensions of whatever narrative intentions precede it. At the same time, however, there must *be* standpoints, because otherwise it would be impossible to write. Towards the end of the novel, Tristram reflects on the mobility necessary if he is not either to subsume his life under a single heading or to give up writing because he has no standpoint to guide him.

I must here observe to you the difference betwixt My father's ass and my hobby-horse – in order to keep characters as separate as may be in our fancies as we go along. For my hobby-horse, if you recollect a little, is no way a vicious beast; he has scarce one hair or lineament of the ass about him – 'Tis the sporting little filly-folly which carries you out for the present hour – a maggot, a butterfly, a picture, a fiddlestick – an uncle Toby's siege – or an *anything* which a man makes a shift to get a stride on, to canter it away from the cares and solicitudes of life – 'Tis as useful a beast as is in the whole creation – nor do I really see how the world could do without it –   (VIII, 31, 476)

To distinguish himself from the obsession of his father, Tristram has to convey to the reader an idea of his own hobby-horse, because this is something he shares with the other characters. The difference between his hobby-horse and his father's is that his is not an obsessive passion but a cheerful whim, a 'sporting little filly-folly', which may lead his attention in this or that direction, enabling him to get away from whatever situation he has been caught up in. The examples Tristram gives bear witness both to the mobility and the discontinuity of his references, as well as to the fact that there is no overall point of view from which they may all be encompassed. Indeed this is already clear from the fact that he confesses to having a hobby-horse himself, thereby downgrading himself to the same level as the other characters. He actually speaks of himself as one of the characters, and so eliminates the seemingly irremovable distance between himself and them; he is the same as they, in that writing about his life can be nothing more than a hobby-horse. On this he rides into life, and the 'beast' is useful because it enables him at least to try to map out his life. The contours that he draws, however, can never be more than hobby-horsical aspects, as is indicated by the fact that they cannot coalesce into a complete picture. And this is why Tristram distinguishes between his own hobby-horse and the continuous obsessions that constitute the world views of the other characters. His hobby-horse highlights the fact that he is just as much exposed to life as the other characters, and also that writing needs standpoints whose discontinuous multiplicity spotlights the lack of a grand-stand view. The apparent absence of a structuring focus gives rise to a continual shifting of perspective views, the fanning out of which into a never-ending sequence makes the inaccessibility of the narrator's life palpable. As the spectrum of perspectives continues to expand, it translates the life that defies comprehension into a continual outgrowth which is only to be grasped as a happening.

Tristram's segmented mode of writing springs from his efforts to depict life as a being in the 'middle of things', and the resultant experience is bound to have consequences both for him and for 'his' characters. For life is not an abstract entity to which they are all exposed; it is they who produce what they have to live through. And herein lies a dilemma which affects narrator and characters in various ways. By means of interruption Tristram gives presence to life in his writing, which, in turn, is meant to capture it. But it appears that life can only be depicted by way of its constant evasion of representation. Now this runs counter to all expectations of representation, which normally signalises something significant. Tristram, too, is concerned with meaning, for that is why he writes, but he does not want to establish it before he writes; his concern is to *find* it. The strategy of interruption enables him to unfold life as a happening, but at the same time it prevents him from translating this happening into a meaning, for if he did so, life would then stand for something which it is not. This dilemma gives a double-edged impetus to the strategy of interruption, in that the interruptions convey the truth of life as a happening but at the same time prevent it from being captured in any meaningful form.

The far-reaching consequences of this type of writing become apparent when viewed from the angle of the characters, whose conduct endows the novel with its dramatic quality. For the eccentric subjectivity embodied particularly by Walter and

Toby is exposed to a 'happening' reality which the characters are quite incapable of perceiving because of their total absorption in their own world. The happening continually passes them by, even though they intrude on it just as frequently as it intrudes on them.

Historically this marks a radical break in the relationship between hero and world in the novel. In *Tristram Shandy* they are both indifferent to one another, but this disjunction between subjectivity and reality is necessary if the former is to be presented as itself, i.e. is to be its own reference and not a sign of something else, as was automatically the case with the heroes of eighteenth-century novels. For only through this complete abstraction from reality as it happens – which the characters themselves produce by way of their idiosyncrasies – can a self-referential subjectivity open itself up to observation. Imperturbable familiarity with oneself simply could not be conveyed without the continual changes of a happening reality which always affects the characters, but which they never really register, let alone process. Processing requires attitudes to be adopted and stances to be developed in order to come to grips with what is going on.

This is tantamount to saying that the subjectivity Sterne reveals in *Tristram Shandy* does not feature as the great challenger to the philosophical systems he caricatures; while the deconstruction of Lockean empiricism renders subjectivity readable, the latter has to be made problematic if it is to be experienced.

This is achieved by way of the gulf yawning between self and world, opened up by the strategy of interruption, which brings about a double-edged relationship between characters and reality: they shut out reality, and that makes them comic, because what does not exist for them will strike back without their even realising it. This gap is different from the one Tristram produces through his writing. A self which is unaware of the difference between itself and the world becomes comic because it does not know that its self-centredness arises not least out of the gulf separating it from any reality outside itself. A self, however, which is conscious of that difference becomes melancholic, because it knows that its singularity arises out of an unbridgeable distance from its own life. If subjectivity appears comic at one moment, and melancholic the next, then the difference responsible for the divergent manifestations requires processing, which takes place through the humour of the novel.

3 Digression

The strategy of interruption indicates the extent to which Sterne reflected through his narrator on narrative techniques. The strategy of digression, which structures the whole novel, is meant to lay bare the narrative fabric. Critics took note of this very early on, and it was of particular interest to the Russian formalists (Shklovsky, 'A parodying novel: Sterne's *Tristram Shandy*', p. 69). The disclosure of techniques runs counter to conventional expectations and causes a shift in focus allowing the object to be separated from its mode of depiction. The Russian formalists therefore believed that such a disclosure resulted in a protracted perception, and hence a prolonged viewing of the object concerned. *Tristram Shandy* certainly did not aim at a revolution of perception, but brought to the fore something that the tradition of the novel had never taken cognisance of: the losses produced by narration. Even disclosed techniques have a history. It is necessary to quote in full the central passage on digression in order to spotlight the multifarious implications that underlie this strategy:

For in this long digression which I was accidentally led into, as in all my digressions (one only excepted), there is a master stroke of digressive skill the merit of which has all along, I fear, been overlooked by my reader, – not for want of penetration in him, – but because 'tis an excellence seldom looked for, or expected, indeed, in a digression; – and it is this: That though my digressions are all fair, as you observe, – and that I fly off from what I am about, as far and as often too as any writer in Great Britain; yet I constantly take care to order affairs so, that my main business does not stand still in my absence.

I was just going, for example, to have given you the great outlines of my uncle Toby's most whimsical character, – when my aunt Dinah and the coachman came across us, and led us a vagary some millions of miles into the very heart of the planetary system: Notwithstanding all this you perceive that the drawing of my uncle Toby's character went on gently all the time; – not the great contours of it, – that was impossible, – but some familiar strokes and faint designations of it were here and there touched in, as we went along, so that you are much better acquainted with my uncle Toby now than you was before.

By this contrivance the machinery of my work is of a species by itself; two contrary motions are introduced into it, and reconciled, which were thought to be at variance with each other. In a word, my work is digressive, and it is progressive too, – and at the same time.

This, Sir, is a very different story from that of the earth's moving round her axis in her diurnal rotation, with her progress in her elliptic orbit which brings about the year, and constitutes that variety and vicissitude of seasons we enjoy; – though I own it suggested the thought, – as I believe the greatest of our boasted improvements and discoveries have come from such trifling hints.

Digressions, incontestably, are the sunshine; – they are the life, the soul of reading; – take them out of this book, for instance, – you might as well take the book along with them; – one cold eternal winter would reign in every page of it; restore them to the writer, – he steps forth like a bridegroom, – bids All hail, brings in variety, and forbids the appetite to fail.   (I, 22, 62f.)

Digression as the main technique of depiction applies to several levels of the novel, which we shall separate for the sake of clarity. For the reader's expectations, for characterisation, and for the narrator these digressions fulfil different functions, although these are so interlinked that the technique works like a single ingeniously geared machine.

The reader must not overlook or underestimate what can be achieved by digression. He will be used to, and will expect, the straight line of the traditional narrative, but he will not find it here. On the contrary, as Tristram stresses many times, his writing aims at swerving from the straight line. This is evident from the typographical patterns he uses to illustrate his meandering procedure (see VI, 40, 385). If we take the reader's traditional expectations as the point of reference, then the problem raised by many Sterne critics – namely, that one can only talk of digression if one knows what is being digressed from – simply disappears. The 'deviations from the straight line' (I, 14, 36) generally invoke the reader's predisposition, with its 'vicious taste' of 'reading straight forwards, more in quest of the adventures than of the deep erudition and knowledge which a book of this cast, if read over as it should be, would infallibly impart' (I, 20, 52). Since the digressions in *Tristram Shandy* are not departures from a (non-existent) line, but are to be viewed as running counter to narrative linearity, their nature – and Tristram himself has no doubts about the importance of his 'digressive skill' – must be quite different from what we normally understand by the term. The negative slant disappears the moment digression is no longer geared, let alone subordinated, to the inherent teleology of the narration.

This is why from the very start Sterne refuses even to hint at any overriding purpose in his novel. Once the tyranny of teleology has been overthrown, the proliferation of digressions reflect the resultant, explosive multifariousness of life. In other words, the digressions compensate for all the losses resulting from the linearity of narration by highlighting what such a depiction of life is bound to exclude.

Historically speaking, the wildly proliferating digressions are Sterne's challenging response to the biographical form of the eighteenth-century novel, which eclipsed everything not intrinsically relevant to the hero's pursuit of self-perfection. Sterne releases life from this strait-jacket. This is his reaction to the same stylisation of human nature which, at around the same time, was leading Horace Walpole to set human nature in extraordinary conditions, thereby giving rise to the first, epoch-making Gothic novel.

Digression, however, is more than just a historical response to the impoverishment of life produced by the hero's pursuit of self-perfection. Having been freed from subservience to the plot-line as a journey, it now takes on the function of structuring life itself. It has to replace the time-honoured pattern inherited from Cervantes. If life unfolds itself in digressions, then it is present as the intersection of infinitely varied presuppositions and their results. As reflected in the digressions, it is a constantly shifting differential between the contingency of actualised potentials and their still unforeseeable consequences. Digressions at this level cease to be 'deviations from the straight line', as they were in relation to consolidated expectations, and instead become a strategy for the representation of events. The event defies referentiality as it transgresses rules and shatters expectations, issuing forth into incalculability. Thus, by replacing the journey as the plot-line, digression enables life to make itself present as a discontinuous sequence of events, refusing to allow the drawing of any connecting thread.

As a strategy of writing and a pattern of experience, the digression is far more than just a historical response to the shortcomings of the eighteenth-century novel. Its prime function, however, in terms of the novel itself, lies in the workings of characterisation and of time as conceived of by the narrator. When Tristram maintains that the digressive movement of his work is also progressive, the latter movement clearly cannot be measured against the continuity of the narrated story, which is prevented by the former. Tristram in fact is referring to what he calls the 'main business' of his digressions, which is 'the drawing of my uncle Toby's character'. This, then, is the progress, and the imagery of the passage quoted is in itself revealing, for he compares (albeit negatively) the simultaneous double movement of his text to that of the earth round the sun. Progression, as R. Warning points out, is not 'the *straight line* of I. 14, but a circular movement. And *digression* here is not the *deviation from a straight line*, but, in astronomical terms, is the respective distance of the earth from the sun, and so is identical to *progression*' (Warning (1965) p. 23). It is true that Sterne calls this image 'a very different story', but Tristram confesses that 'it suggested that thought', and his desire to imprint the metaphor on his reader's mind becomes evident in the way he continues it, comparing his digressions to the sunshine, and their absence to cold eternal winter. In the circular movements of the planets, progression and digression coincide, and so in *Tristram Shandy* digression is no longer a matter of deviation, but is to be seen as concentric rotation around a fixed point, which is the desire to portray uncle Toby's character. It is clear that if the character is no longer the bearer of a meaning, he cannot be brought to life through the progression of a story; instead, the mode of description must tally with the self-relatedness of the character. And as the characters are all distinguished by their singularity, presenting them through a story would lead to eternal winter, because instead of a development the hobby-horses would have produced nothing but endless repetition. Characterisation through digression, however, is sunshine, for it runs a concentric course round the fixed point, which it illuminates from ever changing angles. Since the characters themselves are incapable of change, it is the writing that must move, and it is this method of unfolding character that makes the digressive technique progressive.

The hobby-horse that uncle Toby mounted with such pleasure carried him 'so well, – that he troubled his head very little with what the world either said or thought about it' (I, 24, 67). It is, however, impossible to go riding without coming into contact with the world, and so Toby's singularity is exposed to a multitude of changing situations. Although these are always confronted in accordance with the character's inclinations, they nonetheless reflect the many aspects of the singularity that confronts them. The hobby-horse thus reveals itself by the impact it exercises. But as all the characters ride their own hobby-horses, they each form a world for one another that lies beyond their own singularity. When explaining his strategies, Tristram had already stated that the contrary movements of progression and digression were synchronised through the 'machinery' of his work, emblematically represented by the Shandy family:

Though in one sense our family was certainly a simple machine, as it consisted of a few wheels; yet there was thus much to be said for it, that these wheels were set in motion by so many different springs, and acted one upon the other from such a variety of strange principles and impulses, – that though it was a simple machine, it had all the honour and advantages of a complex one, – and a number of as odd movements within it as ever were beheld in the inside of a Dutch silk mill.   (V, 6, 291f.)

The hobby-horses 'interlock' like the wheels of a machine, but as each singularity is foreign to the other, they produce (paradoxically, in view of their expected reactions) continually unforeseeable situations. For when one meets the other, he automatically subsumes him under his own obsession. It is scarcely surprising that the wheels of such a machine constantly grind out uncontrollable realities, with the self exposed to what it has brought forth, yet totally unaware of the ensuing precariousness. This actually means that subjectivity is divorced from the life which it produces. This life in turn reflects the subject's lack of access to himself, so that subjectivity becomes its own trap, which the characters themselves cannot see because they are too busy riding their hobby-horses, but which the reader *is* aware of through his own laughter.

Digression as a mode of characterisation is Tristram's justification for claiming that 'By this contrivance the machinery of my work is of a species by itself.' The characters circle like satellites, but when they meet, they race off in opposite directions. This is happening all the time, and so the novel unfolds as a sequence of contingent situations overshooting any organising pattern, because those who produce it constantly relapse into their unfathomableness. Therefore the machine of Sterne's work is a *perpetuum mobile* of happenings.

So far we have viewed the digression as a way of shattering the reader's consolidated expectations, of experiencing reality as a happening, and of conveying the impenetrability of subjectivity. In each case, imposed or existing boundaries are transgressed. There is one more boundary which the narrator has to cross, and that is time.

Tristram Shandy must surely be the first novel to attack the substantialist concept of time; instead of time mastering the narrator, he endeavours to master it. Once again this takes place through the digressions:

> when a man is telling a story in the strange way I do mine, he is obliged continually to be going backwards and forwards to keep all tight together in the reader's fancy – which, for my own part, if I did not take heed to do more than at first, there is so much unfixed and equivocal matter starting up, with so many breaks and gaps in it, – and so little service do the stars afford which, nevertheless, I hang up in some of the darkest passages, knowing that the world is apt to lose its way, with all the lights the sun itself at noonday can give it – and now, you see, I am lost myself! – (VI, 33, 377)

The metaphor is one of light rather than time, but since world-time is derived from the sun, the implication is the same – that world-time cannot orientate life-time. One's own life-story emerges, therefore, from the links between what is and what was, and if Tristram regards this as a 'strange way', it is because he and his characters 'instead of living in a present which has references to the past only as the plot requires it, live in a present which derives its character and manifestations entirely from the past' (Baird, 'The time-scheme of Tristram Shandy and a source', p. 317).

In more situations than one Tristram is present in terms of his memory, which always brings together past and present, thereby endowing the past with something it could not have had at the time. In its turn, the present is equally affected by the evocations of memory, and thus carries the latter into a future towards which the present moves. It is therefore scarcely surprising that Tristram finds his hands full, with 'so much unfixed and equivocal matter starting up, with so many breaks and gaps in it'. The breaks and gaps that have arisen during the link-up between past and present trigger a recasting of the lived-through past, thereby moving the present into a continually changing setting. This back and forth movement occurs in the conscious mind, which is a constantly shifting point of intersection between before and after, and thus individualises subjectivity in proportion as the subject links up past and present. While subjectivity produces its own time, its temporality is a sign of how it shapes itself. To articulate this process requires deliberate interventions into chronological, historical and narrative time, which Tristram sets himself to undertake in an all-out effort.

As far as chronological time is concerned, nearly all critics have noted that

The clock's inexorable pendulum has stopped, and now it is the consciousness that has begun to swing back and forth, according to other rhythms than those dictated by an ideal mechanism that could never go wrong, and recording Time elsewhere than on a dial arbitrarily divided into strictly equal sections.

(Fluchère, *Laurence Sterne: From Tristram to Yorick*, p. 95)

With regard to measurable time, it is no longer a question of dividing it differently – instead it has to be chopped up if it is to set off the temporality of the subject. Measurable time runs forwards, which is contrary to the time of the subject. For his time is not a linear movement, but is a ceaseless re-emerging of the past from whatever may be the standpoint chosen in the present. Digression, then, is no longer deviation, but as a wrecker of linear time signalises subjectivity as 'comprehensive' time, i.e. as an unending interpenetration of past and present.

Walter Shandy is an involuntary victim of this process. 'It is two hours, and ten minutes, – and no more, – cried my father, looking at his watch, since Dr Slop and Obadiah arrived, – and I know not how it happens, brother Toby, – but to my imagination it seems almost an age' (III, 18, 152). This intrusion by subjective time into chronological time immediately requires 'a metaphysical dissertation upon the subject of *duration and its simple modes*' (III, 18, 152) so that the phantom character of subjective time may be exposed by the 'mensurations of the brain' à la Locke. This, however, cannot remove the impression that imagined time is more plentiful than measurable time. In relation to the former, the latter seems relatively empty, for chronological time is external to man's life and so can show nothing except its own impersonal flow. The fact that time can run at different speeds amazes Walter, and the attempt to unify different experiences of time by measuring the brain is another instance of subjectivity, as is Tristram's digression from linear time to a constant swinging between present and remembered past.

Through the handling of historical time, subjectivity assumes yet another nuance. Baird, in reconstructing the time-scheme of the novel, came to the conclusion that '*Tristram Shandy*, far from being a wild and whimsical work, is an exactly executed historical novel' (Baird (1980) p. 335). However, if this is so, it is scarcely due to the sequence of historical data rearranged by Baird. A historical novel communicates history by refracting it through the experiences and sufferings of its characters. In *Tristram Shandy*, historical events are at best refracted through the narrator, though he does not experience history for himself but simply reproduces Toby's historical experiences. But even Toby does not experience history in the true sense, for his reliving of military campaigns is more like compulsive repetition than remembered history. In such reproductions of a past event, the processing of the past is obliterated to the same degree as the present which has been momentarily taken over by the past. Time has simply disappeared from Toby's life, and this is true even when he relives the battles of the War of the Spanish Succession in a parallel action. Consequently, time can only make itself felt as a disturbance. The events surrounding the siege of Dendermond move so swiftly that the allies scarcely leave Toby enough time 'to get his dinner' (VI, 8, 345), and when he starts on his egg for supper (VI, 35, 380) he must at once return to the advance into the heart of France if he does not want to lose his thread. Such a reproduction of history manoeuvres Toby into an extraterritorial position in relation both to his present and his memory.

Tristram, however, remembers Toby through his reproduction of battles and campaigns, which now bear witness not to historical events but to the memory of the narrator, who brings into the present a history that took place before his birth. This history now seems to be in utter confusion, and the jumbled events and inverted chronologies manifest the wilfulness of a memory imprinted by the subjectivity of the narrator. Memory is a subjective faculty anyway, and has to enlist the imagination when the past is evoked, especially when the remembered past lies beyond the life of the person recalling it. And so, the more memory fragments past sequences into pointillistic discontinuity, the more unmistakable is its subjectivity, as well as the fact that subjectivity is only present to itself through memory.

There is one more instance of adumbrating subjectivity by digressing from a logical time-sequence of narration. The constant interventions of the narrator are not intended to break illusions in a novel in which disclosure of applied techniques is standard practice. Instead, Tristram interferes in an un-precedented manner by noting events as having happened, though at the given time they have not. For example, he reports:

As Susannah was informed by an express from Mrs. Bridget of my uncle Toby's falling in love with her mistress, fifteen days before it happened, – the content of which express Susannah communicated to my mother the next day, – it has just given me an opportunity of entering upon my uncle Toby's amours a fortnight before their existence.   (VI, 39, 383)

Such an inversion of narrative time evinces more than just the author's taking liberties with his own product. The author already knows his story, and so for him the chronological sequence of events is always overshadowed by the time of their reproduction. If the narration is to be complete, both times must come into play, and so there is a digression from the time of the story to that of the actual narrating – sequence and anticipation interpenetrate. As the narrator swings backwards and forwards between past, present and future, he liberates time from the constraint of succession, and demonstrates that in the last analysis temporal relations are merely organisational forms created by the mind.

Now if Bridget knows about a development that only takes place fifteen days later, this information makes the narrator dependent on his characters, though according to all traditions of narration he ought already to know all about them. Such blind spots make it all the more necessary that – while the narration is going on – the time in which it occurs should be explored so that the operations of the mind may be brought to light. This is why Tristram frequently halts time in his stories, as well as telescoping them together.

In I, 21, 56 Toby takes his pipe out of his mouth in order to say something, but Tristram does not let him say it until II, 6, 83. There are many such instances, and so it is only to be expected that Tristram himself should think about this and forestall any possible criticism. During the two minutes and thirteen seconds that Obadiah needs to return to Shandy Hall with Dr Slop,

I have brought my uncle Toby from Namur, quite across all Flanders, into England: – That I have had him ill upon my hands near four years; – and have since travelled him and Corporal Trim, in a chariot and four, a journey of near two hundred miles down into Yorkshire; – all which put together must have prepared the reader's imagination for the entrance of Dr. Slop upon the stage, – as much at least (I hope) as a dance, a song, or a concerto between the acts.   (II, 8, 86f.)

Tristram condenses a very long period of the past into a very short period of the present, and compares this temporal sandwich to a musical composition, with the interlude, of course, being vastly longer than the acts that it joins together. With this massive disproportion, subjectivity demonstrates its sovereignty over time. The musical analogy for these telescoped stories imposes on time a pattern in which chronological distortion gives way to the simultaneity of different times. But this simultaneity is only made possible by narration, and so the running together of different events and of different durations gives presence to a subjectivity whose idiosyncratic character takes shape through the composition of time. The reader's imagination is essential, because it has to view the different times simultaneously, together with the mind that is reflected through these interpenetrating times.

Here, as elsewhere, the narrated stories digress from one another, and there is no single story as a thread from which others digress. But since all the stories are digressions, because each one has its own time, their telescoping together involves an activity of the mind which seeks to ensure its own singularity by transforming sequence into simultaneity. The time of the conscious mind lends itself to such manipulation as it originates in consciousness which, in turn, allows subjectivity to stage itself by means of self-produced time. This, however, clashes with narrative time, which has to be punctured so that the time of subjective consciousness can become apparent. Thus, permanent digression turns out to be the vital counter-movement through which writing defends itself against the narrative process.

The final question concerning this obsessive preoccupation with digression is what actually drives it along. It springs initially from the unbridgeable gap between staged time and real time. Tristram is a virtuoso at controlling the former, while the latter mercilessly streams away. Right from the start he talks of how little time there is, for instance, to look into all the archives, and indeed 'I declare I have been at it these six weeks, making all the speed I possibly could, – and am not yet born' (I, 14, 37). Occasionally one glimpses the pressure, when, for example, Tristram admits that he had only wanted to leave his father lying on his bed for just half an hour, and thirty-five minutes have already gone by (III, 38, 189). This self-irony as regards the ebbing of time fades away towards the end of the novel. In the last book he ponders upon the survival of his novel, and confesses:

for what has this book done more than the Legation of Moses or the Tale of a Tub, that it may not swim down the gutter of Time along with them? I will not argue the matter: Time wastes too fast: every letter I trace tells me with what rapidity Life follows my pen; the days and hours of it, more precious, my dear Jenny! than the rubies about thy neck, are flying over our heads like light clouds of a windy day, never to return more – everything presses on – whilst thou art twisting that lock, – see! it grows grey; and every time I kiss thy hand to bid adieu, and every absence which follows it, are preludes to that eternal separation which we are shortly to make. –   (IX, 8, 496f.)

When the focus is on real time, the voice of Sterne begins unmistakably to speak through Tristram. Over the heads of his characters the author addresses the mysterious Jenny on the subject of the remorseless flow of time, which threatens his book, like so many other things, with destruction. At such moments Tristram clearly becomes the mouthpiece for his author, who seeks to defy the boundaries drawn round human life. Fluchère is surely correct when he says that Sterne 'writes in order to observe himself living, to watch himself out-living himself, transcending his own existence by an ideal victory over Time' (Fluchère (1965) p. 129). Even if this purpose offers a plausible explanation for Tristram's manipulation of time, what actually fuels the motor of digression is the subject's inability to catch up with himself.

The denaturing of historical time makes subjectivity present to itself as memory; the staging of narrative time gives it presence as consciousness. These modes of self-presentation – brought about by digression – are highly ambivalent as they are not only deviations from historical and narrative time, but equally deviations away from what subjectivity is, and into the time of history and narration. This indissoluble duality of encountering oneself by means of deviations turns digression into permanence, for there are no limits to the self-enactment of subjectivity through memory and consciousness. And this also means, in turn, that subjectivity can never be completely captured by the modes through which it is given presence to itself. If it were identical to any one of its many manifestations, it would be extinguished, and therefore digression becomes a necessity. Subjectivity cannot apprehend itself by re-enacting itself; hence it becomes an endless digression from itself and at the same time towards itself – a countervailing movement which makes it dramatic in terms of the novel, and indefatigable in terms of experience.

4   Equivocation

If depiction is to be permeated by such a vigilant consciousness as Tristram's, then writing itself has to come under scrutiny. Writing as representation always eclipses what is not to the purpose, and these displacements have to be reinscribed into writing if the life Tristram wants to present is not to turn into a sign for something other than itself. Tristram is at pains to recover what his own words tend to exclude, and whenever he does so, that which has been said is bound to change. If language is to be related to life, it must be equivocal, because life eludes semantic pigeon-holing. Words take on their meanings through usage, and each use excludes all others. If usage congeals, language loses its flexibility, as is evident from the behaviour of the characters. But if words are capable of different usages and hence changes of meaning, then simul-taneous usage of different meanings will serve to bring out the multifaceted nature of phenomena. This is all the more necessary because the characters are totally insensitive to the opaque nature of the world around them, which Tristram has to bring to life by means of his equivocal mode of writing.

However, as he cannot continually talk with tongue in cheek – which would inflate the meaning of all words – he exemplifies equivocation by means of paradigms such as whiskers, but-tonholes, chamber maids, chapter divisions, and, above all, sexuality. Sterne's treatment of such matters has often been regarded as a mere whim – to be excused on biographical grounds – as it appears to mar the narrative. And indeed these predilections may well have had a personal reference, but that does not invalidate their significance in bringing to the fore what prevailing conventions had hitherto sacrificed. The eighteenth-century novel, based on the hero's journey to fulfilment, had always ignored matters trivial and matters physical. The hero's quest for perfection allowed no dwelling on superficialities, and the body was at best spoken of when the hero's moral integrity was being tested by an attempted seduction. In *Tristram Shandy* the description of apparent irrelevancies, and the indulgence in a sexuality usually repressed by the eighteenth-century concept of love as idealised companionship, constitutes far more than the mere eccentricity of its author. Tristram speaks about things that had been unspeakable before, and thus brings a banished life out from behind the façade of ideals, which no doubt suffers damage when invaded by what it had suppressed. For this purpose he develops a strategy which circumscribes impropriety in such a manner that the reader cannot avoid imagining it for himself. Through language the imagination has to be captured while at the same time grasping how language functions, and how – in representing life – language must always mean more than it says. Sterne employs various techniques to achieve this end.

The simplest is direct omission, in order to hook the reader's imagination, simultaneously denying it any options as to what it is to conceive. A typical example is the accident to Tristram's penis, concerning which we are never told precise details, despite the graphic description. It all begins with a lapse of memory, which is already a form of omission in itself: 'The chambermaid has left no ******* *** under the bed', and so she tries to get Tristram 'to **** *** ** *** ******', with the result that the sash-window crashes down upon him, to the accompaniment of Susannah's desperate cry: 'Nothing is left' (V, 17, 307). And yet ''Twas nothing, – I did not lose two drops of blood by it – 'twas not worth calling in a surgeon, had he lived next door to us – thousands suffer by choice what I did by accident' (V, 17, 306). This 'nothing', however, precedes the other 'nothing', and as they both mean something different anyway, both the discrepancy and what is concealed by the 'nothing' set the imagination to work. The imagination is provoked into supplying what the words omit, but even though the omission here is called a 'nothing', the imagination will still try to create a 'something' out of it. (And no sooner has it done so than Sterne plays his next trick, to make the reader laugh at his own creativity: 'Nothing is left, – cried Susannah, – nothing is left – for me, but to run my country. – ') Words replaced by asterisks stimulate the imagination, but at the same time control it. Visualising this indecency is a responsibility offloaded on to the reader.

In order, however, that the reader should not now comfort

himself with the idea that Tristram has simply been accidentally circumcised – which might well have been the impression given – we learn a little later

> that in a week's time, or less, it was in everybody's mouth, *That poor Master Shandy* *** *********** entirely . . . 'That the nursery window had not only ********** *************** *****; – but that ******* *************** *******'s also   (VI, 14, 353)

The father's response is: ' – I'll put him, however, into breeches . . . let the world say what it will' (VI, 15, 354). Tristram attaches so much importance to this decision that he makes this single sentence into a whole chapter, thus once again kindling his reader's imagination.

The omissions in relation to the equivocal 'nothing' at the beginning of the episode are enough to stimulate a whole range of projections, and now the decision to put Tristram in breeches confirms the ideas that have been racing through the reader's imagination. Sexuality, in the words of R. Alter, 'energizes the imagination, invites it to free and rapid play . . . The effect . . . of this elaborate rhetorical strategy is to make the reader Sterne's accomplice' (Alter, *Motives for Fiction*, pp. 96 and 98). The complicity between author and reader lies in the communication of what decorum forbids to be communicated. This circumvention is meant to goad the reader's imagination into giving substance to what has been adumbrated. Sterne's use of the sexual taboo here is a clear instance of the way he initiates his reader into a mode of communication that is integral to his representational purpose. Only the imagery generated by the imagination can bring to life unfathomable subjectivity and also the other mysteries that Tristram suspects to be lurking behind the appearances of things:

> . . . mark, Madam, we live amongst riddles and mysteries – the most obvious things which come in our way have dark sides, which the quickest sight cannot penetrate into; and even the clearest and most exalted understandings amongst us find ourselves puzzled and at a loss in almost every cranny of Nature's works.   (IV, 17, 236)

The degree to which sexuality is a paradigm for communication and not its actual object can be seen from Tristram's reflections on the implications of the Slawkenbergius story. The accident with the sash-window conveyed indecency by means of under-determination. Slawkenbergius's nose, however, stimulates ideational activity by means of over-determination. Both are modes of communication, and they simply activate the reader's imagination in different ways.

Tristram explains that 'before I venture to make use of the word *Nose* . . . in this interesting part of my story, it may not be amiss to explain my own meaning, and define, with all possible exactness and precision, what I would willingly be understood to mean by the term' (III, 31, 175). Defining the word before its use means supplying it with two meanings, for if the meaning is identical to the use, then there cannot be a definition of the meaning anterior to its use. This is without doubt an ironic response to Locke, who believed that the 'imperfection of words' could be cured by strict definition. This is not enough for Tristram. He now begins to hurl himself into the task:

In books of strict morality and close reasoning, such as this I am engaged in, – the neglect is inexcusable; and heaven is witness, how the world has revenged itself upon me for leaving so many openings to equivocal strictures, – and for depending so much as I have done, all along, upon the cleanliness of my readers' imaginations.
– Here are two senses, cried Eugenius, as we walked along, pointing with the forefinger of his right hand to the word *Crevice* in the fifty-second page of the second volume of this book of books, here are two senses, – quoth he. – And here are two roads, replied I, turning short upon him, – a dirty and a clean one; – which shall we take? – The clean, – by all means, replied Eugenius. Eugenius, said I, stepping before him, and laying my hand upon his breast, – to define – is to distrust. – Thus I triumphed over Eugenius; but I triumphed over him as I always do, like a fool. – 'Tis my comfort, however, I am not an obstinate one; therefore
I define a nose as follows . . . I declare, by that word I mean a Nose, and nothing more, or less.   (III, 31, 176)

Tristram's apparent determination to remove the duplicity of which he has so often been accused by means of strict definition now reveals definition as the actual source of equivocalness. From a definition one expects precision, which requires a process of exclusion in terms of the meaning to be ascertained. Exclusion, however, implies that the meaning fixed upon derives its stability to a large degree from the meanings it has eliminated. The more constricted a meaning is, the wider will be the extent of what is not meant. Consequently the definition will eventually reach a critical point at which the desired precision will simply disintegrate, because the many excluded meanings edge into focus and so hit back, as it were, against the definition and bring out its motivation.

Eugenius, as the assumed reader of *Tristram Shandy*, discovers the double meaning of *Crevice*, and the pointing forefinger indicates not only the passage in the book, but also a sexual connotation. The attempt to gain precision turns into an enhancement of the equivocalness. And so Tristram distrusts definition, for this inevitably focuses in due course upon the meanings that were supposed to be excluded.

When Tristram, however, decides to define, his intention could be precisely to bring out what definition is supposed to remove. Thus turning definition against itself is an occupation befitting the fool that Tristram owns himself to be. The result is therefore polysemantic. It would seem that definition presupposes fixed meanings, and so fails to recognise the fact that precision comes about not through definition but through usage. Therefore distrusting definition means freeing language from its scholastic realism – the restrictive identification of words with objects. As long as the reader restricts the meaning of the nose to that of the penis, he is sacrificing the potential polysemantic range of the word – a range which Tristram suggests by his definition of the literal sense, though this function can only be performed because he is struggling against the sexual connotations. But can one really be certain that Tristram's insistence on the literal sense implies nothing more than imagining the other sense? After all, in the Bible noses were an ideal of beauty (cf. Song of Solomon 'your nose is like the tower of Lebanon'), which would certainly not have escaped the notice of the parson Sterne, with his interest in curiosities, so that the literal sense could well be intended to rescue the nose from the sexual references in order to convey mistrust in the imagination.

Be that as it may, Tristram uses the generally recognised duplicity of sexuality as a kind of bait, in order to draw attention to another double-meaning – i.e. that of language. Since what is meant is to a large extent conveyed by what is left unsaid, Tristram is at pains to insinuate the implications excluded by the pragmatic context. It is necessary to adumbrate the tacit dimension within what is said if life is to be properly depicted and not just determined *by* what is said. Any definition, like any pragmatic application, will eliminate the double meaning inherent in language, and indeed neither of these operations would be possible otherwise, for they both require unequivocalness if they are to achieve their respective aims. Hence equivocation must be inscribed into the literal sense as well as into the suggested one if the double meaning of language is to be rescued from the tyranny of the written word. Only in this way can a transcribed life make its presence felt in spite of its representation.

This may well be one reason why in *Tristram Shandy* there is sexuality but no eroticism. If we take eroticism to be sexuality glorified by the imagination, in *Tristram Shandy* there is a clear distinction between sexual allusion in the text and its visualisation by the reader. The sexuality in the text always works through omissions, and it is left to the reader to fill in the blanks. Whatever may have been Sterne's personal attitude towards sex, the aesthetic effect of this strategy is dynamic in the extreme, for it seduces the reader into resolving all the ambiguities and at the very same time being suspicious of his own clarification.

This process has two consequences:

1. Sexuality is a textual game that lures the reader into play, during the course of which he himself is acted upon. In this respect sexuality is a function of the text and not an object of representation; in remaining deliberately implied, it lends itself to a strategic application which prevents it from becoming a sign for something other than itself.

2. As a textual game, sexuality is a paradigm of equivocal writing. It trains the reader always to see and to imagine more than words can say. And as words gain their meaning from what they exclude, attention must be drawn to their semantic adumbrations if language is to embrace the ramifications of life and the mysteries of a self-related subjectivity. Raising the implications to the same level as the utterance produces a form of speech that also incorporates what the concrete, pragmatic context has excluded. This insistence on equivocation, therefore, means that the utterance must stretch out beyond its own boundaries.

So long as Tristram himself is speaking, he can bring equivocation directly into his conversation with the reader. The situation is different, however, with Toby and Walter, whose manner of speech and conduct appears to be the very opposite of double-meaning. They handle language as if they knew the exact meaning of what they say, and they purge language of implications even when they themselves are considering alternative meanings. But as we have already seen, the greater the precision, the more is excluded, and the excluded material begins to grow.

Walter is fascinated by a doctrine emanating from Erasmus: 'My nose has been the making of me.' Of course this passage immediately sets itself against the background previously established by Tristram, so that everything Walter now tries to discover is overshadowed by the earlier duplicity. But Sterne does not make his point exclusively in this manner, for Walter's struggle to find the precise meaning of nose itself produces adumbrations of meaning which, because he is unaware of them, reflect back upon all his efforts. At first he is disappointed 'in finding nothing more from so able a pen but the bare fact itself'. Facts do not satisfy him, because for him only the interpretation of a fact is a fact. He therefore reads the dialogue

over and over again with great application, studying every word and every syllable of it through and through in its most strict and literal interpretation; – he could still make nothing of it that way. Mayhaps there is more meant than is said in it, quoth my father. – Learned men, brother Toby, don't write dialogues upon long noses for nothing. – I'll study the mystic and the allegoric sense; – here is some room to turn a man's self in, brother. My father read on. (III, 37, 185)

This reading, however, now becomes very strange, for Walter

got out his penknife, and was trying experiments upon the sentence, to see if he could not scratch some better sense into it. – I've got within a single letter, brother Toby, cried my father, of Erasmus his mystic meaning. – You are near enough, brother, replied my uncle, in all conscience. – Pshaw! cried my father, scratching on, – I might as well be seven miles off. – I've done it, – said my father, snapping his fingers. – See, my dear brother Toby, how I have mended the sense. – But you have marred a word, replied my uncle Toby. – My father put on his spectacles, – bit his lip, – and tore out the leaf in a passion.

(III, 37, 185f.)

It seems as if Walter wants to dig out the meaning of the word archaeologically. The meaning appears mystic because it is hidden, and he thinks he will be able to uncover it by removing all the debris. For him there should be nothing that cannot ultimately be known, and so what is meant by nose must be knowable. But the more he delves into 'the mystic and the allegoric sense', the more one is tempted to describe his quest in

terms of a pun: 'noses = gnosis'. If 'gnosis' is to be proved by
the study of 'noses', then each will undermine the other: 'gnosis'
will swallow up 'noses', and 'noses' will trivialise 'gnosis'. The
extinguished word will make itself present again as ambiguity.
Its disappearance shows that it has no single meaning of its own
that could give it existence, while its supposed unequivocalness
becomes a trail for all the excluded meanings. This form of
equivocation can only be demonstrated through a character
that is totally unaware of all ambiguities. The fact that such a
character is drawn as a Gnostic makes knowledge equivocal,
and this process is essential if we are to remain aware of what is
lost when life is recorded in writing.

Life can only become present in language if the character of
words is split, for it is their equivocalness that brings out
whatever the pragmatic use has concealed. Double-meaning
restores to life its dynamism, which verbalisation threatens to
destroy. For the more life is subjugated to language, the more it
transforms itself into a sign, and the more the sign splits up into
its duality of showing and concealing, the more life overflows
the medium of its representation. Toby's life is the most obvious
example, and through him we can also discern the variations
offered by sexuality as a metaphor of double-meaning.

Widow Wadman wants to know exactly where Toby was
struck by the splintering stone:

And whereabouts, dear Sir, quoth Mrs. Wadman, a little categorically,
did you receive this sad blow? – In asking this question, Mrs. Wadman
gave a slight glance towards the waistband of my uncle Toby's red
plush breeches, expecting naturally, as the shortest reply to it, that my
uncle Toby would lay his forefinger upon the place – It fell out
otherwise – .   (IX, 26, 517)

For instead of the expected response – either indicating the
place of the body or simply the town of Namur – Toby places
Mrs Wadman's finger on a map,

and with such a virgin modesty laid her finger upon the place, that the
goddess of Decency, if then in being – if not, 'twas her shade – shook
her head, and with a finger wavering across her eyes – forbid her to
explain the mistake. Unhappy Mrs. Wadman! –   (IX, 26, 518)

The fact that Toby guides the widow's finger is no doubt much
to her liking, and since she had already glanced towards the
waistband of his breeches, it may be presumed that this was

where she thought her finger would be laid. But instead of landing on his genitals, it lands on a map. The latter is a very strange signified for such a physical process of designation. Instead of leading to understanding, the semiotics here signifies several ambiguities. Using the map to indicate the place of the wound is both plausible and absurd: plausible, because it demonstrates the eccentricity of subjectivity, and absurd because the map is not the place of the wound. That which is now supposed to be made clear Toby conceals with the map, and in this way his idiosyncrasy makes its mark on the speechless and disappointed widow. She, however, is not entirely blameless for this failure of communication, since she avoided asking Toby directly what she wanted to know. It is only Toby's reaction that brings out the unspoken implications of her utterance. Once again equivocalness springs from the return of what has been excluded, and this arises out of imaginary maps which all of us carry within us in order to pin down the signifiers (cf. Krieger, *Poetic Presence and Illusion*, p. 168).

Toby and the widow act on each other like mirrors, reflecting, as it were, one another's inner view, the virtuality of which cannot be captured by language and so can only be made present through the failure of what is said. The characters themselves remain unaware of this doubling. Their unawareness both of the massive exclusions brought about by their language and of the rebounding of those exclusions on what they think they know makes them into eloquent witnesses of a life that stretches far beyond the bounds of linguistic representation. This virtual life is given shape by the manner in which the reverse side of their conduct and attitudes is continually shown up by the misfiring of their verbal actions.

This toppling of speech corresponds to Tristram's equivocation. Though different, these are two related strategies for unfolding the double-meaning of language in order to make conceivable the tacit dimension inherent in verbalisation. As equivocation overlaps the utterance with its own adumbrations, so what was revealed topples over to uncover what had been shut out. Since the novel sets out to make life discernible through writing, double-meaning has to be brought to the fore and, at the same time, must be dragged into a continual process of inversion.

Chapter III

The play of the text

1 The imaginary scene

A mode of writing which refers to itself as it goes along, and a subjectivity that loses itself in its own unfathomableness, together spotlight the limitations of representation, if the latter is understood in accordance with the mimetic tradition of rendering a given. But the inaccessible may also be a given which equally stands in need of presentation. What remains intangible, however, cannot be imitated, but it *can* be played. For play in the sense of staging is in principle capable of anything. And this is why Tristram regards his narrative not as the reproduction of events, but as a play – and from time to time he reminds his reader of this very fact:

I have dropped the curtain over this scene for a minute, – to remind you of one thing, – and to inform you of another . . . When these two things are done, – the curtain shall be drawn up again, and my uncle Toby, my father, and Dr Slop shall go on with their discourse, without any more interruption.   (II, 19, 118)

Nevertheless, he goes on opening and closing the curtain. As Toby and Walter begin to descend the staircase and pause to carry on the conversation: 'A sudden impulse comes across me – drop the curtain, Shandy – I drop it – . . . and hey for a new chapter!' (IV, 10, 227). And when he wants to do his reader a special favour, his invitation is to 'step with me, Madam, behind the curtain, only to hear in what kind of manner my father and my mother debated between themselves this affair of the breeches, – from which you may form an idea, how they debated all lesser matters' (VI, 16, 354). Directing the characters and presenting them as a piece of theatre has a twofold advantage. Through play it is possible to reach behind the impenetrability of subjectivity, but at the same time the penetration is shown to be nothing more than play. Penetrability therefore undergoes a sort of double coding – it is impossible, but it is also real; impossible, because subjectivity cannot be penetrated; real, because play allows hidden areas of the self to be staged. As staging, the play only has the character of an appearance, though this does not prevent it from being the real bearer of what is staged, for it opens up an otherwise closed world. The latter is, as it were, 'broken open for us and delivered to the spectator, but nowhere does it cross over into the real world – it is not the real room behind a window. One cannot "penetrate" into the inner world, which remains inaccessible, but one can look into it, it allows us an "insight"' (Fink, *Spiel als Weltsymbol*, p. 99).

Transforming epic space into a stage set – as *Tristram Shandy's* theatre imagery suggests – entails a shift in emphasis as regards what narrative literature is usually meant to achieve. The novel had been primarily orientated towards mimesis, presenting a model of a given world. But even if such a model is nothing but a copy, it nevertheless produces its 'image' through an act that is not mimetic but performative. No matter what the concept of mimesis entailed throughout its long history, it could only come about through some kind of production.

Richardson represented a petty bourgeois milieu which served to illustrate a classless morality in order to rearrange the social pyramid of the eighteenth century. Fielding represented human nature, which was to be refined through 'prudence' and 'circumspection' in order to bring about human self-perfection. Smollett represented social structures of the eighteenth-century society, which he viewed critically in order to explore its hidden or unconscious driving forces. Such representation was both mimetic and performative at the same time, with the inherent performance serving to process the world rendered by the novel.

Now when such 'given' realities disappear, and what exists appears to be riddled with mysteries (see IV, 17, 236), representation becomes increasingly performative as opposed to imitative, for it has to produce what is only adumbrated by the characters. This dramatic shift in balance turns representation into play, which as a form of production serves the purpose not of imitation but of discovery. For play entails rooting out the base that underlies the world of the characters, and yet at the same time it constantly overshoots whatever this base appears to be. It is intentional, but it can only achieve its intentions by way of phantasy, and phantasy – though indispensable –

demands freeplay, which always runs contrary to intention-
ality. It is this counter-movement that throws into question
everything that has been produced, and so the product always
has the character of something staged. The novel no longer
imitates a world, but becomes an imaginary set where the
indefinable is acted out. However, as the indefinable eludes
definition, freeplay takes over and constantly undoes what
appears to be a tangible result, thus conveying the indetermin-
able as an experience. The transformation of the novel into an
imaginary set tends to minimise the mimetic component of
representation in order to highlight play as a means of
'*worldmaking*' – which had hitherto not been a prime concern of
narrative (cf. Goodman, *Ways of Worldmaking*).

The imaginary set forces the narrator into a dual role – he is
both actor and director at the same time. While he rides his
hobby-horse (e.g. I, 8, 17), he is like the other characters whom
he presents, but when he presents them, he is outside them.
Thus he is both involved in, and distanced from, himself: he is
able to step out of his subjectivity without ever transcending it.
He is not trapped in his subjectivity, and yet he cannot ever
leave it behind. It is small wonder that he is perplexed when
asked: 'Who are you?' He can only answer: 'Don't puzzle me'
(VII, 33, 425). He hangs between his self and his other self, and
at best one could say that he 'is' the being between the two
selves, but this, of course, is the being that defies definition. His
intermediate position, however, is what enables him always to
be other than what he is at any given moment. This makes him
into the fool that he is forever calling himself, because the fool
embodies 'difference' between the roles to be acted out.
Difference, however, is not a place to linger in, but one which
triggers a constant back-and-forth movement, which indeed is
the basic play movement and features the fool, who keeps
forever moving to and fro, as the player *par excellence*. Play
yokes opposing forces together, and the difference between
these opposites makes them break up into a kaleidoscopic
variety which, in turn, uncovers the elements that had remained
hidden by each position.

The fool, then, gives presence to what had been absent, and
he forces together what seems to be mutually exclusive, such as
subjectivity and the subject's efforts to reach behind itself. He
holds the mirror up to his characters in order to reflect their
reverse side, and between them he opens up different games on

stage. Consequently, the characters become double-faced, and this has repercussions on how one is to perceive them. What appears on stage is now to be viewed from different angles. The nimbly shifting fool is the ideal director to work on the imaginary set arranged for his characters, for he always duplicates everything and thus ensures that perception will never remain stable.

2   The games played

On the imaginary set the various games of the characters take place, thereby unfolding the 'dramatic' structure of the text. 'How my uncle Toby and Corporal Trim managed this matter, – with the history of their campaigns, which were no way barren of events, – may make no uninteresting underplot in the epitasis and working up of this drama. – At present the scene must drop, – and change for the parlour fireside' (II, 5, 82).

If Toby's replayed campaigns are the 'underplot' of the drama staged by Tristram, then they, too, must comprise an imaginary set which will be reflected by the drama in which it is embedded. But all

play scenery naturally always [needs] real space and real time in order to be able to unfold itself in the first place – but space *in* the play world and time *in* the play world never spill over into the surrounding space and the surrounding time. On the basis of the fragments of space and the fragments of time that function simply as bearers of the play world, there arises the imaginary scene with its inner space, which is nowhere and yet is there, and with its inner time, which is nowhen and yet is now. And even the player is through his role marked off from the context of the rest of his life.   (Fink (1960) p. 234)

The 'bowling green', just like the days that Toby and Trim spent there, forms the playful scenery which is situated in real space and takes up real time and yet remains radically separate from the reality that repeatedly takes place within it. Thus the minimal properties of reality clearly show up the ineradicable difference, though this is to be glossed over by the play, while at the same time they are the real bearers of the play and so endow the production with the appearance of reality. The play is presented as a break with reality, but only so that it can become that from which it marks itself off. The same applies to the players. The more Toby merges into his role, the more irrevocably his life is transformed into an underpinning of this role-playing, which borrows its reality from the life it has subjugated to itself. Thus what the novel as an imaginary scene picks out by way of the actors in play is their effort to transform play into reality, in order to regain what the play itself has excluded.

Toby is different from Walter in that quite literally he plays. In his 'apologetical oration' he frankly admits:

If, when I was a schoolboy, I could not hear a drum beat, but my heart beat with it – was it my fault? – Did I plant the propensity there? – did I sound the alarm within, or Nature? When Guy, Earl of Warwick, and Parismus and Parismenus, and Valentine and Orson, and the Seven Champions of England were handed around the school, – were they not all purchased with my own pocket money? Was that selfish, brother Shandy? When we read over the siege of Troy, which lasted ten years and eight months, – though with such a train of artillery as we had at Namur, the town might have been carried in a week – was I not as much concerned for the destruction of the Greeks and Trojans as any boy of the whole school? Had I not three strokes of a ferula given me . . . for calling Helena a bitch for it? Did any one of you shed more tears for Hector? And when King Priam came to the camp to beg his body, and returned weeping back to Troy without it, – you know, brother, I could not eat my dinner . . . And heaven is my witness, brother Shandy, that the pleasure I have taken in these things, – and that infinite delight, in particular, which has attended my sieges in my bowling green, has arose within me, and I hope in the corporal too, from the consciousness we both had that in carrying them on, we were answering the great ends of our creation.   (IV, 32, 375f.)

It may at first seem strange that the peace-loving Toby should regard war games as the aim of creation. The series of examples that he gives, however, amounts to the oldest of all games – contest, fighting, or *agon*. It is a matter of winning, and this is why Toby loses his appetite over defeat.

At this juncture we should glance briefly at the different categories of play to be distinguished in the text. The terms used by Caillois (see Caillois, *Man, Play, and Games*, p. VIII), which have now become standard in game theory, are: *agon, alea, mimicry*, and *ilinx*. (There are other less common forms which we shall also be referring to in passing.) *Agon* is a fight or contest, and is a common pattern of play when the text centres on conflicting values. *Alea* is a game based on chance and the unforeseeable, its main textual thrust being defamiliarisation. *Mimicry* generates illusion, whether depicting a world as if it were real, or – when punctured – turning that world into a mirror image of the referential world outside the text. *Ilinx* is a game which subverts, undercuts, cancels or even carnivalises the various positions as they are played off against one another.

Ever since his schooldays, Toby seems to have had an almost Heraclitean feeling for agonism as the father of all things. But if *agon* is the basic game, this does not mean that Toby plays it; he only mimics it, i.e. *agon* is the subject of the game which is played as *mimicry*. This form of game

> presupposes the temporary acceptance if not of an illusion, then at least of a close conventional and in certain aspects imaginary universe. The subject makes believe or makes others believe that he is someone other than himself. He forgets, disguises or temporarily sheds his personality in order to feign another. (Caillois (1961) p. 19)

Now Toby is certainly not aware that in replaying the campaigns in Flanders and the battles of the War of the Spanish Succession he is feigning to be someone other than himself. On the contrary, if he has any consciousness at all of his situation, at best it is that through such games he can be exactly what he is. For this is where his hobby-horse can gallop unhindered – not least because the *mimicry* game embraces all the qualities of every game – 'liberty, convention and suspension of reality and delimitation of space and time' – while at the same time not demanding that which governs all other games, namely 'the continuous submission to imperative and precise rules', for these could not apply to the 'substitution of a second reality' (Caillois (1961) p. 22) as produced by *mimicry*.

This substitute reality is not, however, entirely without rules, for the course of the imitated war is something given, the re-enactment of which is left to the discretion of the player. Hence the rules operative in the game are not regulatory but 'aleatory', allowing what is given to be played subjectively. Thus to play *agon* by means of *mimicry* according to aleatory rules appears to be the triumph of gaming. Now, what is that gaming meant to achieve? This question is all the more essential if we bear in mind that the game is supposed to highlight the very purpose of creation.

Like every other play, this one has an imaginary setting which permits illumination of the subject-matter to be re-enacted. In the real military campaigns, Toby and Trim were little fish in a big pond which they could never see as a whole. Now they are giants, striding the bowling green, actively participating in the miniature battles they stage. The town they have constructed

> was a perfect Proteus – It was Landen, and Trerebach, and Santvliet, and Drusen, and Hagenau, – and then it was Ostend and Menin, and Aeth and Dendermond. – Surely never did any TOWN act so many parts, since Sodom and Gomorrah, as my uncle Toby's town did. In the fourth year, my uncle Toby, thinking a town looked foolishly without a church, added a very fine one with a steeple.
>
> (VI, 23, 365)

The freedom granted by play is also apparent in the *mimicry* of the individual actions. In the real siege of Namur, Toby had been struck in a vital place by the splintered wall, while after the real battle of Landen, Trim had lain for one and a half days wounded on the battlefield before being rescued along with thirteen or fourteen others (VIII, 19, 462). Now, however, in acting out all these events, they are free to play all the parts they had been unable to play at the time: generals, defence strategists, quarter-masters, advisers, and even true philosophers of war, as when Toby reflects:

> For what is war? . . . when fought as ours has been, upon principles of *liberty*, and upon principles of *honour* – what is it, but the getting together of quiet and harmless people, with their swords in their hands, to keep the ambitious and turbulent within bounds?   (VI, 32, 376)

Mimicry, then, is not mere repetition, but goes far beyond that which it repeats, in order to possess all those aspects that could not be possessed at the time. It grants simultaneous personal involvement in the events and absolute sovereignty over them. In their guise as actors they can act out everything that the real situation had denied them, and so the imaginary scene created by them exposes the hidden aspects of that reality they re-enact. And in this sense they typify a basic pattern of the whole novel.

With the smooth transition from the Flanders campaign to the War of the Spanish Succession, Toby's passion for gaming tends to become an end in itself. The *mimicry* is no longer a matter of simply repeating his own experiences – now he applies himself to what he had *not* experienced. He would love to have been there, as is evident from his shining enthusiasm as he reflects whether to go and fight against the Turks under Prince Eugene (VI, 12, 351) – but it is clear that nothing remains to him except his passion, though this is boundless enough to enable him to play the scenes that fill his imagination.

The Peace of Utrecht is therefore a bitter blow for his *mimicry*, and consequently he now appears 'so naked and defenceless . . . (when a siege was out of his head)' (VI, 29, 372) that Tristram hastens

to . . . clear the theatre, *if possible*, of hornworks and half-moons, and get the rest of his military apparatus out of the way; – that done, my dear friend Garrick, we'll snuff the candles bright, – sweep the stage with a new broom, – draw up the curtain, and exhibit my uncle Toby dressed in a new character, throughout which the world can have no idea how he will act.   (VI, 29, 371)

If the world has no idea what Toby's new role is to be, then expectations may be raised, or raised expectations may be thwarted. How is Toby suddenly to change? It is typical of Tristram's equivocal mode of writing that he both raises and ruins expectations, for hardly has he changed the scene on his stage when along comes Widow Wadman '[who] basely patched up the peace of Utrecht' (VI, 30, 373) in order to draw Toby into a love-war. This, however, ends – without a peace treaty – with the widow's finger placed on a map and pointing to Namur. In between there are lost battles, though these are not won by Toby either. He has just made his proposal of marriage, when

casting his eye upon the Bible which Mrs. Wadman had laid upon the table, he took it up; and popping, dear soul! upon a passage in it, of all others the most interesting to him – which was the siege of Jericho – he set himself to read it over – leaving his proposal of marriage, as he had done his declaration of love, to work with her after its own way.
                                        (IX, 19, 516)

In the love-war Toby does indeed take on a new role, but it is only the situation that has changed, and now he applies his internalised *mimicry* from a different situation to the new one, and consequently fails. And yet at first sight his habitual game does not seem altogether inapposite when applied to the love-war, since this doubtless contains its own element of *agon*. But his *mimicry* of battles and campaigns is by now so predominant that every situation is subjected to the stylisation of the game. What he had originally gained from acting out his own experiences – namely, the enjoyment of experiences he had *not* had – now overflows into all the situations Toby finds himself in, ranging from the love-war to all the relationships in Shandy

Hall. The new role into which he was cast after his war games had been terminated turns out to be nothing but an ironic gesture of Tristram's, indicating that if playing epitomises one's attitude towards the world, one cannot help losing the game.

Thus the function of play for depicting subjectivity moves into focus. According to Caillois, *mimicry* embodies a form of play in which the player uses a disguise in order to shed his conventional self, thereby setting free the individual and perhaps even the true personality (Caillois (1961) p. 21). In Toby's case, *mimicry* can hardly be said to serve the purpose of feigning either a different personality hidden underneath the assumed role, or one from which he wants to liberate himself. He appears, rather, to be a player through and through. However, his gaming arises out of imitating his military experiences as well as other private inclinations, and so the games are not purely an end in themselves but – even if they are a sign of eccentricity – nevertheless contain the basic characteristic of *mimicry*, which is that the mimic leaves himself. But Toby can only leave his singularity, which in its turn is unfathomable. The game, then, is related to and indeed emerges from this unfathomable base. And so it seems to be the only manner in which subjectivity can become present to itself. Being inaccessible to oneself is clearly an intolerable state, and the less aware the subject is of this state, the more evident it becomes to the onlooker such as Tristram and the reader. It is a state that can only make itself felt through an almost manic passion for play, for play is action in which subjectivity forces itself outwards – not in order to lose itself to its own otherness, but in order to stage itself as itself. This is why *mimicry* is the form of play most suited to subjectivity – it permits one to leave one's singularity and to imitate it at the same time, an imitation which never ceases while geared to unfathomableness as evinced by Toby. Play therefore exercises a double function: it enables the subject to break out of his singularity, and through this act of liberation allows himself to possess himself. For otherwise singularity would be unable to free itself from itself unless it became something different, thereby extinguishing itself. This 'having oneself' in play is a state of happiness which permeates the whole of Toby's life, for in playing himself he can simultaneously step out of himself and stay with himself, never being drawn into the conflicts inherent in all relations. Toby in play does not have to create himself as someone else, but instead can possess himself as he is. It may therefore be said that at the historic moment at which subjectivity becomes its own subject-matter, play is shown to be the necessary mode for its manifestation.

Depicting subjectivity as the playing of itself entails presenting it as an unending game. The endlessness is due to the fact that subjectivity in playing itself does not step out of a definable entity but out of its own indeterminableness. Therefore its unfathomable singularity gives rise to a ceaseless playing of itself as all the various manifestations are nothing but flickering shadows, none of which could ever claim authenticity. The individual facets that constantly emerge in the gaming will never coincide with what subjectivity is; instead, all of them are mere images or views of that singularity. Thus many images are possible, and each will mirror a different aspect of the unfathomableness in relation to the situation within which it appears. Like a *perpetuum mobile* subjectivity rotates its way through one image after another, and in its endlessness lies an equal degree of good fortune and bad. Good in that the playful world of subjectivity allows so many variations of how the self may be with itself – Toby, for instance, recovered from his wound in real life, and is able to obtain relief through re-enacting his erstwhile reality. But the ill-fortune lies in the fact that residing in a play-world never allows the self to break free from itself, thus turning the difference between self and world into an abyss.

Tristram demonstrates this variation of the game through his father, who unlike Toby is unaware that he is playing. Instead of replaying reality, he believes that he can master it by his theories. Walter therefore conducts the conflict between self and world under his own conditions of play. The substance of Toby's game was *agon*, which he played according to *mimicry*, and *agon* also provides the basis for Walter's play, but this is always encroached on by another substance which Walter himself does not wish to be confronted with. This is *alea*. In *agon*, 'the player relies only upon himself and his utmost efforts' (Caillois (1961) p. 44), as he strives to defeat his opponent. Walter's opponent, however, is reality, and to defeat that would entail removing the difference between self and world, and making subjectivity into the world. Right to the end of the novel, this is his firm intent: 'to force every event in nature into an hypothesis, by which means never man crucified TRUTH at the rate he did' (IX, 32, 523) (see also VI, 36, 381).

Walter is truly the Don Quixote of *Tristram Shandy*, though in him only the manic elements of the knight are filtered through, for in his conflicts with reality he excludes his opponent, despite the fact that he needs him (or rather it) in order for his theories to gain any purchase. Reality challenges him, and so he must fight it, with the intent to eliminate the very thing that conditions his philosophy. So that the struggle should not be totally phantasmal, the excluded opponent takes up his position in the game – and determines its content – in the role of *alea*. The fact that chance now takes over the game makes itself known to Walter even to the extent of inflicting physical pain upon him.

What a chapter of chances, said my father, turning himself about upon the first landing, as he and my uncle Toby were going downstairs – what a long chapter of chances do the events of this world lay open to us! Take pen and ink in hand, brother Toby, and calculate it fairly – I know no more of calculations than this baluster, said my uncle Toby (striking short of it with his crutch, and hitting my father a desperate blow souse upon his shinbone), – 'Twas a hundred to one – cried my uncle Toby. – I thought, quoth my father (rubbing his shin), you had known nothing of calculations, brother Toby. – 'Twas a mere chance, said my uncle Toby – Then it adds one to the chapter – replied my father. The double success of my father's repartees tickled off the pain of his shin at once – it was well it so fell out – (chance! again) – or the world to this day had never known the subject of my father's calculation – to guess it – there was no chance.   (IV, 9, 226)

Walter's philosophy is agonistic, in that it combats the intrusions of reality upon his self-enclosed world, but as chance continually invades this enclosure, he is forced to play the game of *agon*, at the same time generating *alea* as its subject-matter. For *alea* is a game

based on a decision independent of the player, an outcome over which he has no control and in which winning is the result of fate rather than triumphing over an adversary . . . In contrast to agōn alea negates work, patience, experience and qualifications. (Caillois (1961) p. 17)

Indefatigably Walter continues to play *agon* against *alea*, but not only does he have no prospect of winning; he himself is also played with by the very opponent that he is seeking to defeat. Chance takes over the contest, and so the outcome of the struggle must remain permanently unforeseeable, for although Walter cannot win, he will continue to compete.

Now under such circumstances, subjectivity ought to become

aware of itself. But if it did, it would enter into a relationship with itself, and this would entail a view from outside the self. Playing, however, is an activity that allows the self to stay with and within itself, whereas if the subject were to enter into a relationship with himself, the self-containment of the self would be ruptured. Furthermore, playing offers a variety of ways in which singularity may be fanned out into many different nuances. Playing *agon* as an involuntary generating of *alea* is certainly different from having *agon* as the substance of playing *mimicry*. Play endows subjectivity with an opportunity to manifest itself; but the manner of gaming gives an individual slant to what is common to all subjectivity. Therefore the combination of games serves to bring out the idiosyncratic features which can assume inalienably bizarre shapes when games are played against their grain or have their structures inverted when they are combined. Playing *agon* as an involuntary generation of *alea* in order to endow the struggle with a purpose – namely, to control chance – makes the game endless, but by doing so it proves that nothing can break up the self's being with itself. This is why Walter's 'whole life [is] a contradiction to his knowledge' (III, 21, 163), though the consequence is that his knowledge is also played according to the conditions of chance.

Walter's game of playing the elimination of the chance that he himself keeps producing leads to the continual loss of the mastery he seeks, so that eventually it is the player himself who is constantly being played. This game brings out the gulf that extends between self and world – a gulf which Walter always thinks he can bridge by means of his theories. It is a game played involuntarily by the player against himself and thus reveals ineluctably how impossible it is for subjectivity – even when it supposes itself to be active – to step out of itself.

Much as Walter and Toby resemble each other in this respect, they are definitely distinguished by their modes of gaming, which individualise what they have in common. Both are players who present their subjectivity by means of different surrogates, which are both a substitute for and a pointer to subjectivity's otherwise impenetrable base. Playing, then, results in a constant generation of surrogates which allow for the self to act out staying with itself without ever defining what eludes definability. It therefore issues into an unending variation through which the singularity of the self emerges.

During the Romantic period this endlessness is endowed with
the aura of infinity as the distinguishing attribute of the self.
Sterne, however, plunges it into comedy, thus indicating that
endless gaming is but a 'supplement', at best a role by means of
which subjectivity can only play its inability to grasp itself and
make itself available to the world. For this reason Toby lives
only in his 'supplements', which he constantly spins out of
himself, while Walter is continually forced to undo his 'supplements' in order to replace them with new ones which then suffer
the same fate. Walter's games are freeplay, through which the
unforeseeable always comes into being; Toby's games arise
from the illusion that by playing them he can regain the basis of
himself, and this is why he equates his games with the goal of
creation. Thus their games move in radically different directions, though neither of them knows what he is actually
bringing into play. Walter's freeplay leads to a continual
overshooting of what it has achieved, which is certainly not his
intention. On the other hand, a game that expects to uncover
origins remains pure pie in the sky – hence the fantasy of re-
enacting war as the assumed end of creation. And so, while both
players nearly always stand virtually together throughout their
quests, they are almost infinitely distant from each other as
well, for they represent the two poles of play – freeplay, and the
restoration of a whole. And as all their games take place on the
imaginary set devised by Tristram, their play enables subjectivity to be differentiated.

Now as we have seen, Tristram himself rides a hobby-horse
as well, so that he too must play himself if he is not to make
subjectivity into something other than game-playing. There is
no single concept of play that can subsume both freeplay and
the restoration of that which cannot be grasped, but as the
director of his own theatre, Tristram cannot indulge exclusively
in either the one or the other form of play. His game must
achieve two things: it must elucidate that of the other characters, and it must elucidate him in play. Therefore he cannot play
the games of his characters, for otherwise he would coincide
with them, and yet in his game he must so outstrip that of the
others that he will become a kind of framework for them while
at the same time objectifying himself. And so Tristram does not
play *agon*, or *mimicry*, or *alea*, or any of their possible
combinations, but *ilinx* – a form of play 'based on the pursuit of
vertigo and which consist[s] of an attempt to momentarily

destroy the stability of perception . . . this vertigo is readily linked to the desire for disorder and destruction' (Caillois (1961) pp. 23f.) and – one should add – leads to a form of carnivalisation such as lends itself particularly to the fool which Tristram sees himself as. *Ilinx* has an anarchistic tendency which releases things suppressed, and when it is played by the fool it is guided by an awareness that is not without rules. Even though Tristram does not feel bound to 'any man's rules that ever lived' (I, 4, 12), the vertigo into which he plunges everything is guided by an aleatory rule which juggles subjectively with all traditional forms, generic possibilities, and rhetorical tropes.

The rule is aleatory in so far as the inherited plethora of forms and conventions is now played according to subjective standards and not those which formerly determined their application. Lanham correctly points out: 'Sterne's innovations do not stand within the range of expectation realistic fiction holds out. He did not extend the domain of the novel. Much rather, he appropriated its subject for an elaborate game with classical narrative patterns. These are rhetorical, nonmimetic, nonrealistic' (Richard A. Lanham, *'Tristram Shandy': The Games of Pleasure*, pp. 27f.). For Tristram feels himself called upon to juggle with traditions and conventions in an aleatory manner, by means of which he creates himself, only to plunge the resultant objectification into a dizzying dance of forms, thus highlighting the fact that *ilinx*, the game played by him, is nothing but a 'supplement' of his own ungraspable subjectivity. In order to grasp himself, he is continually driven into freeplay which entails the undoing of what has been achieved. By simultaneously carrying out the two counter-movements of play, Tristram becomes the total player, and is able to depict himself so long as his principal strategy is that of *ludus*. This incorporates 'calculation, contrivance and subordination to rules', unlike *paidaia*, 'which is active, tumultuous, exuberant and spontaneous' (Meyer Barash in his introduction to Caillois (1961) p. VIII). Although his game contains elements of *paidaia*, these serve him to increase the cleverly reasoned-out dominance of *ludus*, sometimes in precisely the same way as freeplay pushes his *ilinx* game to its very limits. Thus a heightened sense of self-awareness permeates Tristram's gaming which, however, aims at giving free rein to an unbridled phantasy.

This also entails Tristram playing *against* the other games of the text, not least because in his role as fool he has erected the imaginary set on which Toby and Walter act. This proves to be not merely a stage-world on which the protagonists are presented, but also, through the counter-movements of the various games, the means of depicting what cannot be defined cognitively – namely, subjectivity. In this process, Tristram fulfils an important function: when he plays *ilinx* according to the strategy of *ludus*, his play throws into relief the structures of the other games, which spotlight singularity as an individualis-ation of subjectivity, including his own, which, in turn, is refracted through the mirror of the other games. But his game also refuses to yield 'a single point of view in the novel, a philosophic control as it were, and then continually alerts us to the need for one. Thus we must constantly search for a key, a basis for interpretation, and feel silly for doing so' (Lanham (1973) p. 98). For cognitively inaccessible subjectivity, which can only be revealed through the individualising 'supplements' brought about by the game played, there can be no subsuming concept, even though we are continually provoked into search-ing for one. And if indeed we do feel silly for doing so, this feeling reveals the ineradicable difference which makes singu-larity what it is.

Tristram as the central subjectivity of the novel – central because it registers everything around it, including its own impermeableness – has set up the imaginary scene, but as he acts on it just like everyone else, he is also reflected by it. But in his case, what is mirrored forth is not that which has remained concealed, as with the other characters; instead, Tristram himself is staged by his author in the form of a hologram. For the reader is confronted with images from various angles – the *ilinx* player is Tristram's self-carnivalisation; the stage-director is the opponent of the characters he directs; the fool interprets subjectivity as a game; the narrator blots out all points of view. Holographically Tristram comes and goes through the aspects from which he is seen, and thus he becomes a figure of play pure and simple, because playing *with* him always coincides with being played *by* him.

Tristram Shandy is, then, the embodiment of what is virtually total play. No matter what individual definitions of play one might offer, it will always produce something, even when it is only concerned with re-enacting given realities. Performance is its keynote, and its elevation in *Tristram Shandy* shows clearly that this novel relies predominantly on performance and not on mimesis to divulge its reality. This reality is subjectivity, which is only to be grasped through exploration and not imitation. Play is the mode of its presentation, which tilts the balance in favour of the performative element, which is always present, even when it is subservient to imitation in the concept of mimesis. The further a pre-given object fades from view, the more important performance becomes in setting the intangible before the reader's imagination. Instead of mimesis, play now becomes the backbone of representation. This is clearly to be discerned by the absence of plot and story, which as causal and sequential organisation of narrative have always underpinned mimetic intentions. Their place is taken by the unconnected games of the hobby-horses, through which subjectivity is presented as an endless iteration of its aspects, making its inaccessible base emerge through reactions that are both expected and yet at the same time surprising; thus Sterne avoids the potential tedium of subjectivity for ever playing itself.

Play as an all-pervading feature in *Tristram Shandy* fulfils two divergent functions at the same time: it presents subjectivity and thematises its own mode of presentation, in consequence of which it highlights subjectivity as an object of exploration, and all the findings as nothing but 'supplements'. Hence only gaming renders subjectivity tangible. If what one is can only be played, then what one is, is inextricably equivocal. It is this equivocalness that gives rise to Sterne's humour.

3 The humour

In 1752 Fielding wrote: 'Of all the Kinds of Writing there is none on which . . . Variety of Opinions is so common as in those of Humour, as perhaps there is no Word in our Language of which Men have in general so vague and indeterminate an Idea' (Henry Fielding, *The Covent-Garden Journal* I, p. 249). Obviously, the theory of humours fell short when it came to explaining the form of humorous writing that gradually emerged in the first half of the eighteenth century. Humour was no longer to be equated with the four constitutive elements of the human body, but had become a form of comedy independent of, though related to, other branches such as wit, satire, and irony. The range of comedy had broadened out in the eighteenth century, far beyond its traditional borders, and

so at the time when Fielding assessed the situation, it had indeed
faded away into an indeterminate idea. But this was before
Tristram Shandy came on the scene.

The prevailing concept of humour at the end of the
seventeenth century may be summed up in Dryden's remark:
'That which makes a humor ridiculous is its singularity' (quoted
by Tave (1967) p. 123). It is a comment that might almost be
applied to Sterne, except that for Dryden it had a different
meaning. Singularity seemed ridiculous to him because it
embodied a deviation from the type, but also because its
presence did not represent anything. 'To Dryden humor is an
oddness that begets malicious pleasure in the audience' (Tave
(1967) p. 100), and so at best it is 'satirist's carrion' (Tave (1967)
p. 104). As long as the type was a yardstick, all peculiarities
counted as comic, but during the first half of the eighteenth
century more and more emphasis came to be laid on the
individual, and so the type became more and more the comic
figure, not least because his representative function was increasingly obliterated by the changing circumstances of life. Malicious comedy changed its target, although the individual was
not spared completely. When he was attacked, however, it was
only mildly, mainly because the very variety of singularity did
not allow for such blatant exposure as had been the practice
during the reign of the type. When the individual was comic, it
was less because he had lost his representational function than
because his singularity showed the same lack of flexibility as
made the type look ridiculous. The individual therefore had to
be trained to use his faculties properly, and particularly to
develop his 'good-nature' – that birthright of eighteenth-
century individuality. Comedy was a necessary part of this
process, for it presupposed that the individual was capable of
correction; comedy always incorporates a pattern of restitution, since it promises that all contradictions, inconsistencies
and deficiencies will be made good in the end. Unlike satire,
which seeks to demolish its object with a view to preserving or
resurrecting the ideal, the comedy aimed at the eighteenth-
century individual was intended to heal the split between
singularity and reality. In both cases it articulated difference
together with the attempt to remove difference. If the type was
meant to triumph, difference lay between abstract ideality and
empirical reality; if the individual was meant to be educated,
difference lay between singularity and reality. If neither of these

opposed positions gave way to the other, then reality had to be so inscribed into the individual that he became aware of his singularity. Whatever its contents, this kind of comedy aimed at sparking off awareness, for the latter was considered to induce self-correction. This could come about through wit, satire or irony, each of which brings into play the intellectual element of comedy, whether through surprising combinations, potential ideals or detection of difference in feigned agreement.

It is difficult, however, to equate humour with this tendency. Humour seems above all to lack the comic pattern of restitution. It does not right wrongs. 'The humorists', writes Tave, 'have an individuality as detailed and strikingly vivid as their creators can fashion. Their claim to universal significance rests less and less, in the later eighteenth century, on their being representatives of a species, manner types, and more on their uniqueness' (Tave (1967) p. 167). Exalted singularity, then, is the source of humour, whose comedy arises neither from failure to measure up to the ideal nor from the individual's need for correction, but from ineffable individuality itself. Humour, therefore, is the characteristic sign of subjectivity, and so as a form of comedy it only became possible at the moment when the individual was discovered as subjectivity. Therefore Fielding's description of humour as 'vague' and 'indeterminate' was, in 1752, absolutely right, for another seven years were to elapse before Sterne began *Tristram Shandy* and, at the same time, launched the humorous depiction of the subjectivity he had discovered. One might indeed argue that without subjectivity there would be no humour, and without humour, subjectivity could not be grasped. Since the latter is humorous, and humour is a form of comedy, clearly the difference which lies at the centre of comedy now shifts into subjectivity itself, which can no longer be measured against ideals or against reality, but only against itself. As Jean Paul writes in his *School for Aesthetics*:

For every humorist the self plays the first role; when he can, he even introduces his personal circumstances upon the comic stage, although he does so only to annihilate it poetically. The humorist is both his own court jester or quartet of masked Italian comedians and at the same time their prince and director. The reader must at least bring no hatred but some love for the writer's persona, whose semblance must not be made into being. The best reader of the best author would be one who could thoroughly enjoy a humorous lampoon on himself.

(*Horn of Oberon. Jean Paul Richter's School for Aesthetics*, p. 94)

If subjectivity embodies itself by internalising the comic conflict, then it will clash neither with ideals nor with reality, but for this very reason it must also forego the possibility of correction. Thus the self-referentiality of subjectivity precludes the resolution of its conflicts. This makes it humorous, and at the same time shows that humour as a form of comedy is no longer concerned with positions but lies in and indeed originates from relations. If humour is traced back to eccentricity, no matter how extreme, this is nothing but a throwback to the tradition that viewed comedy as deviation. Such a view presupposes guidelines which can no longer apply to self-referential subjectivity, and so humour does not highlight contradiction any more, but becomes a medium for the representation of the self's relationship to itself. The comedy therefore lies, as Jean Paul stresses 'never . . . in the object, but in the subject' (Jean Paul (1973) p. 77).

This can be observed on several levels in *Tristram Shandy*. The self-relatedness of the characters discloses itself to Tristram, and his own self-relatedness reveals itself to the reader, who thus plays a part himself in the proceedings and is finally inveigled into playing out his own humorous self-relatedness.

'Everything in this world, said my father, is big with jest, – and has wit in it, and instruction too, – if we can but find it out' (V, 32, 320). The fact that Walter fails to find it out – even if Yorick does consider him to be inspired for having such an insight – is due to his total identification with his hobby-horse. This is a phantasm which both Walter and Toby spin out of themselves in equal measure.

When the self identifies totally with the phantasm, it may initially appear to have eliminated the difference between self and world; but in actual fact the split has now moved into the self – thereby sealing it off from its base, which it believed it had regained by identifying with the phantasm; in consequence of this, the base is irredeemably lost. There is no mysterious power that has robbed subjectivity of its base; the loss is self-inflicted, since the self has fossilised itself in its phantasm.

But as the various hobby-horses unerringly lead their riders into trouble, one would have expected the self to become aware of its entrapment in its own phantasm, and to rescue itself from ludicrousness by breaking the self-imposed spell. Why does this not happen? The protagonists certainly do not see themselves as ridiculous. According to Jean Paul:

[no] man's actions can appear ridiculous to himself, except an hour later, when he has already become a second self and can attribute the insights of the second self to the first. A man can either respect or scorn himself in the midst of an act . . . but he cannot laugh at himself
(Jean Paul (1973) p. 79).

But Toby and Walter's second self of the second hour never gets a chance to revise the views of the first self, because they never cease to ride their hobby-horses. And when from time to time they are thrown, like Toby after the Peace of Utrecht, they obstinately begin immediately to remount. Thus they only appear ridiculous to those who *can* use their own selves to revise the views of Toby and Walter's selves – such as Tristram and the reader, who bring to the fore the comedy of the protagonists' situations.

It is clear that identification with the phantasm typifies these characters, and brings about 'blissful isolation from the world around them', while it also breaks off 'permanently every other possibility of contact' (Hörhammer (1984) p. 127), above all with themselves. This double isolation from world and self makes the characters seem almost infantile, and this was already apparent in the eighteenth century with affectionate references to Toby's 'childlike quality' (see Tave (1967) p. 166), but it also allows the self, trapped in its phantasm, to achieve the otherwise impossible satisfaction of having itself in what it is. Being independent of oneself and undetermined by the world may be madness, but it is also bliss. For Freud this was characteristic of humour:

The grandeur in it clearly lies in the triumph of narcissism, the victorious assertion of the ego's invulnerability. The ego refuses to be distressed by the provocations of reality, to let itself be compelled to suffer. It insists that it cannot be affected by the traumas of the external world; it shows, in fact, that such traumas are no more than occasions for it to gain pleasure.
(*The Standard Edition of the Complete Psychological Works of Sigmund Freud* XXI, p. 162)

One might almost believe that Freud had set out to interpret the main characters in *Tristram Shandy* – a book which we know to have been one of his favourites (see Peter Brückner, 'Sigmund Freuds Privatlektüre', p. 898).

This psychological description of humour, however, focuses on its representational features rather than its inner workings.

Although the search for pleasure is in no way a secret kept from the characters, nevertheless humour cannot be confined to depicting a state of affairs, for here it consists rather in unfolding multifarious relationships. The self becomes a self by drawing certain boundaries; the hobby-horse denotes a boundary not only between self and world but also between self and self.

If, in becoming itself, the subject has to draw boundaries, these automatically entail shutting out what does not belong to the respective manifestation of the self, although the subject has no objective means of deciding what is or is not to be excluded.

Walter and Toby draw their subjective boundaries in accordance with what they think they encompass. For them subjectivity is a form of self-appropriation, in that they project themselves outwards in order to block off experiences that do not fit in with their pattern. But since the subject can become what it thinks it is only by the process of exclusion, it appears humorous, i.e. comic, but implicitly blocking any form of correction.

The idea that the shattering of the spell wrought by the hobby-horse would release the characters from their excessively rigid self-enclosures does not work, as subjectivity emerges for what it is by drawing its own boundaries. If the alternative is only a different type of boundary-drawing, the degree of self-alienation caused by enclosing oneself in one's hobby-horse remains constant, irrespective of what the individual phantasm may be like. The latter, then, only expresses the fact that there is no objective justification for the subjective boundaries, and singularity merely hypostatises this deficiency. The need to draw the boundaries leads to separations of self from self, and so the subject's manifestations must inevitably be distortions of itself. Humour is a kind of symbolic approach to that which eludes representation, for the laughter arises from our supplying that which is missing.

In the last analysis, the subject's boundary-drawing will always be in the nature of trial runs, since there is no objective reference underlying the process of inclusion and exclusion (this problem has been adequately dealt with by Gabriele Schwab, *Entgrenzungen und Entgrenzungsmythen. Zur Subjektivität im modernen Roman*). What the old theory of the humours considered to be a product of nature now becomes the decision of the self, which – though it appears quite arbitrary – is in itself a condition for self-fashioning. What was once determined by nature is now in the hands of the self, whose decisions as to what it wishes to be immunise it against the options of other possible decisions. The rigidity of the chosen form is a subconscious stonewalling against otherness.

'The poet', according to Jean Paul, 'must be able to write backwards, so that his script will be legible in the mirror of art through a second inversion' (Jean Paul (1973) p. 114). This occurs through Tristram, who becomes the 'mirror writing' of the characters he directs. While the other characters, because of their phantasms, are completely enclosed in their roles, Tristram's role is to detach himself from role-playing. (In this connection see the illuminating remarks by Wolfgang Prei-sendanz, 'Humor als Rolle', pp. 423–34.)

What sets him apart is, to use W. Preisendanz's description of narrative humour, the 'projection of a subjectivity which endows its own commitment with the appearance of being uncommitted, and simultaneously exposes its non-commitment as pure semblance' (Preisendanz (1979) p. 432). Underlying this attitude is Tristram's insight that we can only have our lives through their many refractions, or in other words – as already indicated both in the title and the motto – through 'the opinions which floated in the brains of . . . people' (I, 10, 25). Tristram is no exception to this state of affairs, although unlike the other characters he knows that his opinions are only aspects, none of which can ever be identical to what they represent. What the other characters have forgotten – despite the fact that their singularity arises from their individual boundary-drawing and so from their difference, by which they even mark themselves off from themselves – becomes Tristram's obsession: his hobby-horse is to uncover the difference that they have covered up, and he rides it as resolutely as they ride theirs.

Tristram's 'appearance of non-commitment' arises from the fact that he keeps his distance from all that is and all that happens. In novels, the degree of distance regulates the value attached to the facts narrated, but if the distance remains the same, then the significance remains the same, too. This, however, in no way leads to balancing out differences – on the contrary, Tristram's uniform detachment leads to violent swings of the pendulum, as randomness and significance, sentiment and cynicism, the mind and the body, as well as the ridiculous and the pathetic are of equal rank. Tristram's equidistance from things breaks up stabilised relationships and produces a toppling effect, no matter what the content.

He therefore gives up his role of autobiographer and instead adopts the role of detached observer of his own enterprise. He represents no particular view, but is present as the point of intersection for the many views which he articulates in the process of their continual overturning. Each view conditions both perception and concealment of the object it focuses on. It could not, however, be perceived without such views, as there is no such thing as an unmediated grasp of things; it is their overturning that enables perception of those aspects which they have eclipsed. This means that the toppling movement must never end, and so it takes on the eccentricity of a 'humour', and constitutes Tristram's own hobby-horse.

This toppling effect is a basic structure of humour, which according to Jean Paul 'lowers the great. It does so like parody, but with a different goal: to set the small beside the great. Humor raises the small like irony, but then sets the great beside the small. Humor thus annihilates both great and small, because before infinity everything is equal and nothing' (Jean Paul (1973) pp. 88f.). But Tristram's humour has nothing in common with this pathetic infinity, for the latter is, rather, a Romantic projection on to what Sterne discovered as humorous subjectivity. The toppling movement which he sets in motion is related to the depiction of subjectivity which, as we have seen, comes about through the individual drawing of boundaries. Now the complement to the drawing of boundaries is, of course, the lifting of boundaries, and it is this process that depicts the individualisation of subjectivity. Tristram, in running as it were counter to the other characters, acts as a boundary-lifter. He breaks down the restrictions of the phantasm. In this respect he is the 'mirror-writing' of the characters he writes about. But in the context of their rigidity, his removal of boundaries is equally excessive. Instead of self-enclosing, Tristram indulges in unbounded self-dissociation, which is the reverse side of his mobile stances and which he continually overturns in order to prevent the obliteration of the difference between life and its depiction in the act of representation. Thus Tristram becomes a 'comic actor', because he 'must renew and maintain every minute the contrast between his consciousness and his act, even if both are merged in the eyes of others' (Jean Paul (1973) p. 114). He can only do this by distorting the traditional authorial function as he unceasingly overturns what he produces, for only through the counter-movement of covering and uncovering can subjectivity be made present through the story of its life. That, however, means that neither consciousness nor self-reflexivity could solve the problems which the characters create for themselves through their behaviour. If they could, then consciousness or self-reflexivity would provide the pattern of restitution concomitant with the comedy which they produce, and Tristram would have no further part to play. But instead, he remains the fool who, 'without himself having a character must be the representative of the comic mood', for he is 'the true God of laughter' (Jean Paul (1973) p. 116). The self-reflexivity of the fool simply testifies that other patterns of behaviour are possible, but these will also exclude something that will once more demand to be included. Subjectivity thus makes its presence felt – as we have already noted – through its changing boundaries, but these also imprison it within itself and continually make it elusive to itself, since the exclusions will insist on fighting back. Through self-reflexivity Tristram captures the alternation of boundaries being imposed and being lifted, and thus he uncovers what the boundaries had covered. The greater the awareness, the clearer it becomes that subjectivity is performative, for it emerges as a continual self-fashioning. The variability of the boundaries denotes the individuality of the boundary-maker, and this endows Tristram himself with a variety of individualities.

As we have seen, there are no particular guidelines orientating the boundary-drawing, and this very lack makes the characters appear eccentric in the sense of being decentred. This applies especially to Toby and Walter, but also to a lesser degree to Tristram himself, whose eccentricity consists in undercutting what conventions had stabilised. However different the various eccentricities appear, they are, in each instance, a trace of the impenetrable base out of which arises the impulse of drawing and lifting boundaries which, in turn, make the base tangible by either self-enclosure or self-dissociation respectively. It follows that subjectivity, as its own boundary-maker and -lifter, can never fail, for there is no criterion against which boundary-drawing and boundary-lifting is to be measured. This is clear from the conduct of the characters, whose eccentricities lead them to almost continual clashes with everything they have excluded, and yet who remain quite undamaged by the collisions. This is also true of Tristram, who remains unscathed through the boundlessness of this 'toppling'. The impossibility of failure, however, is accompanied by the equal impossibility of success, for if subjectivity provides its own restrictions and de-restrictions, it can never be completed. For self-fashioning always entails a loss of other selves, and indeed that is the price that must be paid for any *Gestalt* of subjectivity. Tristram is aware of this, and tries to minimise the loss by means of his toppling, the result of which, however, makes the price appear inflationary.

All this turns Tristram into the 'mirror-writing' of his author, thus exposing the humorous nature of subjectivity. The humour both resides in and reveals the fact that subjectivity in fashioning itself through the imposition and lifting of boundaries always leads to the eclipse of what it is. What makes subjectivity humorous is its barred access to that which brings about its manifestations – indeed, it actually causes this inaccessibility either by self-enclosure or by self-dissociation, thereby turning itself into something separate from itself. In the attempt to be itself, subjectivity creates its own unavailability. The comedy generated through this endeavour is such that it denies the possibility of solution normally inherent in comedy. For there is neither an ideal of subjectivity, nor a concept of its potential totality against which the various manifestations might be measured either as fragments or as failures. It is precisely because there are no such references that subjectivity becomes a game of boundary-drawing and boundary-lifting, with each *Gestalt* continuing a kind of victory that is based on an equal measure of defeat. Humour signalises the defeat within the victory, and communicates the ineradicable ambivalence of subjectivity, which wins and loses but equally defers the final solution we expect of comedy. In its humour, then, subjectivity is 'imposing judgement on itself' (Wolfgang Preisendanz, 'Manuskript' zum 60. Geburtstag von W.I.).

In subjectivity, Sterne has uncovered the hidden dimension of Locke's philosophy. By doing so, he simultaneously reveals subjectivity as the condition of its own transformation, the humorous unfolding of which reveals that being oneself entails foregoing any external reference as well as recovering the base out of which the self had arisen. In this respect, Sterne outstrips the eighteenth-century enthusiasm which acclaimed the individual's coming to himself as the epitome of self-realisation.

Humorous subjectivity, on the other hand, undercuts this assumed perfectibility, since for Sterne individualisation of subjectivity is an unending process of decentring oneself. Therefore subjectivity can never become its own ideal, and so its socialisation becomes a problem. Sterne tackled this by linking social integration to man's innermost feelings, and in doing so he provided a historical answer to the question which humorous subjectivity left trailing in its wake. In the second half of the eighteenth century, feelings embodied an ultimate, non-repressive totality which could embrace what in the field of cognition had split up into contradictory propositions. The counter-movement of the self between covering and uncovering, imprisonment within one's own phantasms, or being the intersecting point of one's own potentials – those were all paradoxes puzzling reason and understanding but accessible to the emotions. The counter-sense of humour, which could encompass all these countervailing moves, facilitated a kind of play of the emotions, which could also cope with the eccentricities of subjectivity playing, fashioning and losing itself. Through feelings, Sterne was able to counter the inaccessibility which subjectivity created for itself, and in this sense humorous subjectivity is historically conditioned. These historical features, however, are by no means so dominant that they prevent Sterne's discovery from attaining validity far beyond the period of its genesis. But if at times feeling lapses into sentimentality in *Tristram Shandy*, this indicates the pressure exerted by the historical situation, which he countered through imbuing humorous subjectivity with tearful tenderness.

In one respect, however, the significance of emotion has outlasted the historical situation it dealt with: as sympathy, emotion forms a central precondition for the reception of humorous subjectivity. For humour only comes full circle by transposing an observing self into humorous subjectivity. At this point we must take a brief look at the historical context.

In the year in which Sterne began *Tristram Shandy*, Adam Smith published his *Theory of Moral Sentiments*, which offered a systematic exposition of sympathy as being a basic category of eighteenth-century feeling. A precondition for sympathy, according to Smith, is the human ability to 'lend' one's own feelings to someone else:

. . . the spectator must, first of all, endeavour, as much as he can, to put himself in the situation of the other, and to bring home to himself every little circumstance . . . He must adopt the whole case of his companion with all its minutest incidents; and strive to render as perfect as possible, that imaginary change of situation upon which his sympathy is founded. (Adam Smith, *The Theory of Moral Sentiments*, p. 21)

This process demands what Smith regards as a characteristic split of the human being into the frequently invoked 'great inmate of the breast', and that part of us which must orientate itself through the 'supposed impartial spectator', for 'it is only by consulting this judge within, that we can ever see what relates to ourselves in its proper shape and dimensions; or that we can ever make any proper comparison between our own interests and those of other people' (Smith (1976) p. 134). It follows that 'The propriety of our moral sentiments is never so apt to be corrupted, as when the indulgent and partial spectator is at hand, while the indifferent and impartial one is at a great distance' (Smith (1976) p. 154). If this faculty of sympathy springs from a doubling of the self, it is nonetheless also dependent on the imagination, which must build the bridges enabling 'exquisite fellow-feeling' to be effective as the foundation of 'Humanity' (Smith (1976) p. 190). But since imagination does not necessarily coincide with moral norms, the split self may get into difficulties, as Smith indicates:

His [i.e. 'the wisest and firmest man's'] own natural feeling of his own distress, his own natural view of his own situation, presses hard upon him, and he cannot, without a very great effort, fix his attention upon that of the impartial spectator. Both views present themselves to him at the same time. His sense of honour, his regard to his own dignity, directs him to fix his whole attention upon the one view. His natural, his untaught and undisciplined feelings, are continually calling it off to the other. He does not, in this case, perfectly identify himself with the ideal man within the breast, he does not become himself the impartial spectator of his own conduct. The different views of both characters exist in his mind separate and distinct from one another, and each directing him to a behaviour different from that to which the other directs him.   (Smith (1976) p. 148)

Now if there are circumstances in which the self can, as it were, fall between its selves, it is clear that the division can be strategically manipulated according to the intention by means of which fantasy – which is free from moral orientations – is pricked into action.

This is the very basis of Jean Paul's theory of humour as practised by Sterne – Adam Smith's contemporary – in communicating with the reader. Jean Paul writes:

When Sancho suspended himself over a shallow ditch all night because he assumed an abyss gaped beneath him, his effort on this assumption was quite understandable. And he would have been truly mad if he had risked being dashed to pieces. Why do we nevertheless laugh? Here comes the main point: We lend *our* insight and perspective to *his* effort and produce through this contradiction the infinite absurdity. Our imagination, which here as in the sublime is the mediator between inner and outer realms, is enabled to make this transfer as in the sublime, only by sensuous clarity, in this case, that of the error. It is our self-deception in attributing to the other person a knowledge and motivation contradictory to his effort which produces that minimum of understanding, that perceived nonsense, at which we laugh.

(Jean Paul (1973) p. 77)

If it is only 'projecting our point of view' (Jean Paul (1973) p. 78) that completes the comedy, then the comic text splits the reader into the self that sides with the characters, and the self that monitors this process of transposition. This doubling of the self corresponds to the required attitude which Adam Smith described in relation to sympathy. But sympathetic transposition into someone else, and the simultaneous orientation of this act through the 'impartial spectator', are guided by moral standards. However, if we 'lend' our sympathising self temporarily to a comic character and thus discover the ludicrousness of the latter's behaviour by relating it to our rational self, our sympathetic division can only resolve the apparent irreconcilability by laughter. But what happens if laughter does not provide the assumed resolution? Then the co-ordination of the sympathetic split collapses by the very reaction to which the comic situation has led us.

The reader of *Tristram Shandy* cannot avoid seeing through the idiosyncrasies of Walter and Toby as they ride their hobby-horses – indeed, as soon as a situation develops, he knows precisely how they will react. In principle, this awareness ought to lead to boredom, but instead its effect is comic. This is mainly because the reader interpolates his own standpoints into the characters' compulsive repetitions, thereby making their deficiencies obvious to himself in his position of superiority. But since the characters are never ruined by their situational failures, they do not seem to notice that anything is wrong. This is why they hardly ever seem ridiculous to one another (cf. III, 24, 169f.), let alone to themselves. In fact, they are immunised against the comedy which the reader wants to force on them, because they think they have precisely the insight which he regards them as lacking. What is this insight? Is it self-awareness that they lack, or is it another form of self-delineation – although Toby, Walter and Yorick already draw completely different boundaries around themselves? What could be the guidelines for 'better' relationships with themselves? The clash between the reader's sympathetic and judgmental selves is reinforced by Tristram's conduct. He has the awareness that the other characters lack, but this does not offer any solution. One might think, then, that Tristram's practice of equidistance, which topples the convention-governed hierarchies of norms and values, is true to life, since everything in life has its own importance which would be underestimated if events were to be subordinated to a system of values from the very start. One might also think that his mode of writing merely embodies a consequence to be drawn from Locke's philosophy, in that the data impinging on the mind make it impossible to know their degree of importance and significance. But if such reasoning were to hold water, Tristram could hardly be comic, for his refusal to regulate distance would then elucidate a plausible insight. But he *is* comic, and this is because of his mania, in his guise as fool, for breaking down all boundaries – a mania that corresponds to that of erecting boundaries, as practised by the other characters who imprison themselves in their chosen phantasms.

Whatever insights the reader might think up in order to correct the behaviour of the characters are wrecked by Tristram, whose mania for breaking down boundaries seduces the reader into a mode of conduct similar to that of the characters. He, the reader, struggles to make sense of the narrator's counter-sensical manner of writing, and so imposes his own ideas. From this process emerge the references that guide the observing self, which then finds itself confronted with the choice between suppressing many of the insights of the self that lends itself to the narrator, or accepting that all its references are pragmatic decisions which, as signs of subjective boundary-drawing, are no different structurally from the hobby-horses of the characters.

If the reader does not wish to fall victim to his own hobby-horse, he must overturn it. For if he has seen through the characters and yet still behaves as they do, then the awareness which he has and which they lack will now be turned against himself, and the only difference possible between him and them will be that he at least has the chance to overturn his own cognitive operations. And this will bring him along the path towards Tristram, though he will probably never catch up with him, because Tristram's counter-sensical mode of writing will never cease to topple whatever solutions the reader may think he has found. In other words, the reader alternates between mounting and falling off his hobby-horse, and so is drawn into the game of drawing and undrawing boundaries which makes humouristic subjectivity into a real experience. 'Attitudes are nothing, Madam; – 'tis the transition from one attitude to another – like the preparation and resolution of the discord into harmony, which is all in all' (IV, 6, 223).

Chapter IV

Epilogue

Despite Sterne's enduring fame and place in the history of English literature, no one has yet written a history of the reception of *Tristram Shandy*. If anyone should undertake it, then it would need to be more than just 'snake-like squiggles to describe the peaks and valleys of reputation' (Max Byrd, *Tristram Shandy*, p. 138). Reception is not orientated solely by prevailing expectations, but also – and sometimes in equal measure – by judgments pronounced in preceding periods which, though more often than not inapplicable, still condition the new question to be asked. Reception always depends upon cultural codes and reactions to past judgments, and from this interplay it is possible to see how the potential of a work has unfolded in the course of its history.

Towards the end of his life, Sterne wrote to an American admirer, thanking him for a walking-stick:

Your walking stick is in no sense more *shandaic* than in that of its having *more handles than one* – The parallel breaks only in this, that in using the stick, every one will take the handle which suits his convenience. In *Tristram Shandy*, the handle is taken which suits their passions, their ignorance or sensibility. There is so little true feeling in the *herd* of the *world*, that I wish I could have got an act of parliament, when the books first appear'd, 'that none but wise men should look into them.' It is too much to write books and find heads to understand them. (Sterne, *Letters*, p. 411)

Evidently his work offers different handles, and one ought to try to grasp them all, not just those which suit one's own disposition. Grasping several handles at once would entail not imposing one's own projections on to the work, but instead allowing the work to correct one's projections. Understanding would then mean absorbing something into oneself that had hitherto not been in the orbit of the reader.

How little attention was paid to these precepts is all too evident from the judgments of such famous contemporaries as

Samuel Richardson. Like many others, the latter praised Sterne's talent for character drawing: 'Yorick, Uncle Toby, and Trim are admirably characterized' – but otherwise his reaction to the various books is: 'execrable I cannot but call them . . . Unaccountable wildness; whimsical digressions; comical incoherencies; uncommon indecencies; all with an air of novelty, has catched [sic!] the reader's attention' (*Selected Letters of Samuel Richardson*, pp. 342 and 341; see also Gerd Rohmann, 'Die zeitgenössische Rezeption (1760–1813)' pp. 19–29). This irritation is tantamount to a confession that fictional characters can be appealing without conforming to the implicit demands of the eighteenth-century novel that they be carriers of moral concerns.

Those more favourably disposed towards Sterne placed him in the great line of Rabelais and Cervantes, seeing him as a satirist. Edmund Burke was one such, though he, too, had his problems with the novel: 'These digressions so frequently repeated, instead of relieving the reader, become at length tiresome': but at the same time the 'faults of an original work are always pardoned' (*Dodsleys's Annual Register* 3 (1760) p. 247). For all his goodwill, though, Burke too was guided by the prevailing expectations as regards the hero of an eighteenth-century novel: he had to represent moral attitudes, and so one must simply tolerate whatever could not be subsumed under that heading.

It is not surprising, then, that quite a few of Sterne's critics were impressed by Yorick's sermon on conscience, which even Horace Walpole – whose judgment was otherwise harsh – singled out for grudging praise: 'The characters are tolerably kept up; but the humour is forever attempted and missed. The best thing in it is a sermon' (*Horace Walpole's Correspondence with Sir David Dalrymple*, p. 66). Since Walpole himself reacted against the moralising novel of the eighteenth century by launching the Gothic novel, in order to free human nature from the constraints of stylisation, his remark here is convincing evidence of what Sterne's contemporaries expected of narrative literature.

That there was something special about Sterne's characters, however, does seem to have been generally noted, even when they were simply dismissed, as in Dr Johnson's grandiose misjudgment: 'Nothing odd will do long. *Tristram Shandy* did not last' (James Boswell, *The Life of Samuel Johnson* I, pp.

618f.). The attacks directed against the book because it
departed from classical novels, as well as from the expected
moral framework, at the same time acknowledged the in-
novatory nature of the characterisation, though this was not
understood, because it demanded new standards of judgment.

Christoph Martin Wieland appears to have been one of the
first to realise this. In a letter of November 13, 1767 – during
Sterne's own lifetime – he wrote to his friend Zimmermann:

I must confess to you, dear friend, that Sterne is virtually the only
author in the world that I regard with a kind of reverential admiration.
I shall study his book as long as I live and yet still not have studied it
enough. I know of nothing that combines so much genuine Socratic
wisdom, such deep knowledge of humanity, such a deep feeling of the
beautiful and the good, such a large quantity of new and fine moral
observations, so much healthy judgment, and so much wit and genius.
(*Ausgewählte Briefe von C.M. Wieland, an verschiedene Freunde
in den Jahren 1751–1810 geschrieben und nach der Zeitfolge
geordnet* II, p. 285)

The moment one penetrates the surface of *Tristram Shandy*, the
criticisms fade away and one discovers the 'Socratic wisdom'
and the human condition. Sentiment and morality are periph-
eral as a means of communicating this insight, and in any
case they are no longer the exclusive topic of a now variegated
reception.

Sterne's reception in Germany was sometimes enthusiastic,
and this had some influence on his growing estimation in
England. It was above all Jean Paul who set Sterne's humour in
a new perspective, releasing it from the satirical and ironic
constraints which such well-wishers as Burke had imposed on
it.

Coleridge attempts to grasp the special qualities of the book
by following the definitions of humour contained in Jean Paul's
School for Aesthetics, at times translating it literally:

The little is made great, and the great little, in order to destroy both;
because all is equal in contrast with the infinite . . . I would suggest,
therefore, that whenever a finite is contemplated in reference to the
infinite, whether consciously or unconsciously, humour essentially
arises. In the highest humour, at least, there is always a reference to,
and a connection with, some general power not finite, in the form of
some finite ridiculously disproportionate in our feelings to that of
which it is, nevertheless, the representative, or by which it is to be
displayed. Humourous writers, therefore, as Sterne in particular,

delight, after much preparation, to end in nothing, or in a direct contradiction. That there is some truth in this definition, or origination of humour, is evident; for you cannot conceive a humourous man who does not give some disproportionate generality, or even a universality to his hobby-horse, as is the case with Mr. Shandy; or at least there is an absence of any interest but what arises from the humour itself, as in my Uncle Toby, and it is the idea of the soul, of its undefined capacity and dignity, that gives the sting to any absorption of it by any one pursuit.

(S.T. Coleridge, *The Literary Remains*, pp. 136f.; see also Jean Paul (1973) p. 88)

For Coleridge, sentiment and decency are no longer the dominant qualities that had guided eighteenth-century reactions to *Tristram Shandy*. With the fading out of the traditional set of values, something else can rise to the surface, and this is the strange doubling of the finite self by an infinite one, together with the self-concealing impulses that go to make up the soul but remain inaccessible to the mind. Precisely because the characters in *Tristram Shandy* no longer function as bearers of meaning, the self is now set free to become its own concern, the multifariousness of which is to be explored. It is humour that provides access to the self, and this mode of access comprises not whimsicality but the strange pathos of infinity which seems to rise up out of the ever widening depth of subjectivity.

Tristram Shandy increasingly becomes a paradigm for the plumbing of the inner man.

A *novel* [wrote Arthur Schopenhauer] will be of a loftier and nobler nature, the more the *inner* and the less of *outer* life it portrays; and this relation will, as a characteristic sign, accompany all gradations of the novel from *Tristram Shandy* down to the crudest and most eventful knight or robber romance. *Tristram Shandy* has, in fact, practically no action at all . . . Art consists in our bringing the inner life into the most intense action with the least possible expenditure of the outer; for the inner is really the object of our interest.

(Arthur Schopenhauer, *Parerga and Paralipomena. Short Philosophical Essays* II, pp. 440f.)

The criticism made in the eighteenth century, especially by Richardson, that Sterne neither told a story nor established coherence, is here taken as a condition for freeing life from all alien purposes of demonstration, so that it can be treated as its own concern.

The history of Sterne's reception was not, of course, a matter of continually revealing the inner workings of the self, as first

came to light through the Romantics, although they were also
partly responsible for the attitudes that coloured nineteenth-
century views of Sterne. For the idea of the poet as genius led to
a mutual intertwining of life and work, each of which was
supposed to mirror the other, and so critics now saw the author
of *Tristram Shandy* as a cloven-hoofed satyr playing his little
jokes.

For Sir Walter Scott, Sterne was 'liable to two severe charges;
– those, namely, of indecency, and of affectation' (Sir Walter
Scott, *The Miscellaneous Prose Works* I, p. 302), a criticism that
was taken and turned into a commonplace by Walter Bagehot,
when he wrote in 1864 that *Tristram Shandy* incorporated
'indecency for indecency's sake' (Walter Bagehot, *Literary
Studies* II, pp. 282–325 made this remark in his review of
Fitzgerald's *The Life of Laurence Sterne*). It was also derided
for those very qualities that Schopenhauer regarded as the
highest art: 'Its style is phantastic, its methods illogical and
provoking' (Bagehot (1916) pp. 282–325) – conditions which
remove the coherence of a story or a plot. Such coherence had
to be preserved, according to an attitude that demanded *high
seriousness* from literature. *Tristram Shandy* was therefore
overlaid by the projections of prevailing cultural codes, whether
they were Dr Johnson's classicism or the Victorians' moralism,
and so it was generally condemned. It refused, however, to go
away, but continued to irritate those who projected their ideas
on to it, for the persistently nagging problem of subjectivity
could not be escaped.

This was a problem which even in the eighteenth century
exercised a profound impact. Goethe was convinced that Sterne
had taken a decisive step towards the discovery of human
Eigenheiten (peculiarities):

there are certain phenomena of humanity that can best be designated
by this term; they are . . . psychologically extremely important. They
are that which constitutes the *Individuum* . . . quite graciously . . .
Yorick–Sterne called these peculiarities 'ruling passions'.
                    (W.R.R. Pinger, *Laurence Sterne and Goethe*, p. 28)

Coleridge endowed these 'peculiarities' with the pathos of
infinity, whose manifestations he considered to be closely
bound up with humour. This remained an undeniable feature to
which even Sterne's detractors had to address themselves, as is
reflected in the reaction of Thackeray, who disparaged Sterne

by denying him the very humour he had been praised for: 'The man is a great jester, not a great humourist. He goes to work systematically and of cold blood; paints his face, puts on his ruff and motley clothes, and lays down his carpet and tumbles on it' (W.M. Thackeray, *The Lectures on the English Humourists*, p. 321). Sterne had to be painted as a slapstick comedian in order to discredit his writing as not being that of a humourist. Nevertheless, Thackeray sensed that Sterne's achievement of tackling subjectivity humorously could only be downgraded by repudiating the humour of *Tristram Shandy*. One wonders whether perhaps this sort of misrepresentation – which also characterises his treatment of other eighteenth-century nove-lists – does not conceal the desire to belittle the predecessors of his own comic mode of writing.

While Thackeray sought to undermine the Romantic recep-tion of Sterne, something similar happened to *his* judgment in the second half of the nineteenth century, as evinced by Nietzsche's appreciation of Sterne. Nietzsche never refers explicitly to Thackeray, and indeed he can hardly have been acquainted with the latter's *Lectures on the English Humourists*, but for this reason his total reversal of Thackeray's line of argument is all the more striking, and is itself evidence of the impact of what Sterne discovered and processed in *Tristram Shandy*. For Nietzsche, Sterne is

the most liberated spirit of his century! . . . in comparison with whom all others seem stiff, square, intolerant and boorishly direct. What is to be praised in him is not the closed and transparent but the 'endless melody': if with this expression we may designate an artistic style in which the fixed form is constantly being broken up, displaced, transposed back into indefiniteness, so that it signifies one thing and at the same time another. Sterne is the great master of *ambiguity* – this word taken in a far wider sense than is usually done when it is accorded only a sexual signification. The reader who demands to know exactly what Sterne really thinks of a thing, whether he is making a serious or a laughing face, must be given up for lost: for he knows how to encompass both in a *single* facial expression; he likewise knows how, and even wants to be in the right and in the wrong at the same time, to knot together profundity and farce. His digressions are at the same time continuations and further developments of the story; his aphor-isms are at the same time an expression of an attitude of irony towards all sententiousness, his antipathy to seriousness is united with a tendency to be unable to regard anything merely superficially. Thus he produces in the right reader a feeling of uncertainty as to whether one is

walking, standing or lying: a feeling, that is, closely related to floating.
He, the supplest of authors, communicates something of this supple-
ness to his reader. Indeed, Sterne unintentionally reverses these roles,
and is sometimes as much reader as author; his book resembles a play
within a play, an audience observed by another audience. One has to
surrender unconditionally to Sterne's caprices – always in the expectation, however, that one will not regret doing so. – It is strange and
instructive to see how as great a writer as Diderot adopted this
universal ambiguity of Sterne's: though he did so, of course, ambigu-
ously – and thus truly in accord with the Sternean humour.

> (Friedrich Nietzsche, *Human, All Too Human. A Book for
> Free Spirits*, pp. 238f.)

The philosopher who spent his life tracing the resentment
and the cultural discontent which he saw concealed in traditional beliefs and contemporary ideas, discovers *Tristram
Shandy* in all the richness of its references. The fractured form
brings out the double meaning, the thwarting of expectations
turns the reader against his own preconceptions, the theatrical
setting permits the staging of what has been hidden, and the
pronounced artificiality of representation makes appearance
into an ultimate reality. In Sterne, Nietzsche finds his most
cherished intentions fulfilled – here is reflected the reverse side
of what is. Something must always be questioned if not
completely decomposed in order to give expression to what
exceeds verbalisation.

Virginia Woolf's judgment sounds almost like an echo of
Nietzsche's: 'In this interest in silence rather than in speech
Sterne is the forerunner of the moderns' (Virginia Woolf, *The
Common Reader. Second Series*, p. 81). Thus Sterne consigns to
history all those nineteenth-century novelists and critics who
had wanted to consign *him* to the past. For the experimental
novel of High Modernism it was he who laid down the
guidelines. If one also takes into account how Virginia Woolf
herself regarded the composition of her characters, then
Sterne's silence assumes its full significance: 'I'm thinking
furiously about Reading and Writing . . . I should say a good
deal about *The Hours* and my discovery: how I dig out beautiful
caves behind my characters: I think that gives exactly what I
want; humanity, humour, depth' (*A Writer's Diary. Being
Extracts from the Diary of Virginia Woolf*, p. 60). What the
characters are made of is hollowed out *behind* them, and so they
cannot be equated with their manifestations. This is in line with

the nature of Sterne's subjectivity, whose duality can only be humorously reflected, just like Virginia Woolf's characters, because their base lies in something that eludes language.

James Joyce moved Sterne's mode of writing into full focus, not – as might be assumed – in *Ulysses*, but in *Finnegans Wake*. 'Have you ever thought of hitching your stern and being ourdeaned' (this and other allusions have been compiled by James S. Atherton, *The Books at the Wake*, p. 123), runs one of the allusions in *Finnegans Wake*, whose subject-matter and complex structure is inspired by *Tristram Shandy*. 'I might easily have written this story in the traditional manner', Joyce told Eugene Jolas. 'It is not very difficult to follow a simple chronological scheme which the critics will understand. But I after all am trying to tell the story of this Chapelizod family in a new way. Time and the river and the mountain are the real heroes of my book. Yet the elements are exactly what every novelist might use: man and woman, birth, childhood, night, sleep, marriage, prayer, death. There is nothing paradoxical about this. Only I am trying to build many planes of narrative with a single esthetic purpose. Did you ever read Laurence Sterne?' (Eugene Jolas, 'My Friend James Joyce', pp. 11f.; see also Robert Gorham Davis, 'Sterne and the delineation of the modern novel' p. 21 and Louis D. Rubin, Jr., 'Joyce and Sterne: A study in affinity', pp. 14–22).

The many countervailing 'planes of narrative' serve to produce an imaginary object which can only come into being through the decomposition of existing conventions. The 'single esthetic purpose' of *Finnegans Wake* may be different from that of *Tristram Shandy*, but in both cases it can only be fulfilled by shattering entrenched representational modes and expectations. What Joyce saw in Sterne was the linguistic capture of what is eclipsed by the representative character of language.

For the most part, the nineteenth century related Sterne's characters and narrative structure to the then prevailing frames of reference, with a view to grasping what Sterne had omitted because it was ungraspable. In the twentieth century Sterne has become a landmark for modern narrative, which removes its own presuppositions in order to speak of what pales into speechlessness, or of what it means when speechlessness breaks into speech. This also requires the use of more than one medium, as we see from the graphs and charts in *Tristram Shandy* and the necessity for the reader to leaf backwards and forwards, thus opening up a spatial dimension within the book itself. Footnotes, diagrams, and the interweaving of a great many different texts function as exemplary signposts to Butor's conclusion that Sterne is 'the greatest artist that I know in the organization of the volume' (Michel Butor, *Inventory Essay*, p. 56).

What Butor regards as a superb achievement had already been noted at the end of the eighteenth century, but then it was considered a serious blemish. The appropriation of other texts in one's own seemed – even to a classically orientated age – to be plagiarism (see among others Richard Cumberland, *Memoirs Written by Himself*, pp. 506f. and Matthew Carey, *Miscellaneous Essays*, pp. 438–46. The first catalogue of other texts to be traced in *Tristram Shandy* was compiled by John Ferriar, *Illustrations of Sterne*), a criticism taken up all too readily by such novelists as Scott (Scott (1854) p. 303), who wished to shed as favourable a light as possible on their own work. But what was then regarded as plagiarism is now conceived as intertextuality, thus evincing that change of perspective in the perception of identical phenomena which is characteristic of all reception. But if the plagiarist Sterne has now been forgotten, that too is evidence that reception can never exhaust the potential of a work, whose total actualisation would allow us at the end (where could that be?) to grasp the matrix out of which the multifariousness of its features have arisen. For reception is a simultaneous process of forgetting and discovering. Indeed, forgetting the plagiarism is a precondition for grasping intertextuality as a means of spotlighting a semantics that speaks of things beyond semantics. But forgetting also entails disappearance from view of aspects of the work that were once regarded as central. These include Sterne's sentimentality and the resultant cult of emotion inspired by it. For current reception, these are past history. But it may be that Sterne's sentimentality, which we have excluded, will be rediscovered some day, although its re-evaluation may then be viewed from yet another angle. It could well be seen as expressing the fact that self-referential subjectivity is permeated by the feeling that it cannot reach itself, thus producing a different cause for sentimentality.

Bibliography and guide to further reading

Alter, R. 'Tristram Shandy and the game of love', *American Scholar* 37 (1968) 316–33.
  Partial Magic. The Novel as Self-Conscious Genre, Berkeley 1975.
  Motives for Fiction, Cambridge, Mass. 1984.
Anderson, H. 'Answers to the author of Clarissa; theme and narrative technique in *Tom Jones* and *Tristram Shandy*', *Philological Quarterly* 51 (1972) 859–73.
  '*Tristram Shandy* and the reader's imagination', *PMLA* 86 (1971) 966–73.
Atherton, J.S. *The Books at the Wake*, London 1959.
Avedon, E.M. and Sutton-Smith, B. *The Study of Games*, New York and London 1971.
Bagehot, W. *Literary Studies* II, ed. R.H. Hutton, London 1916.
Baird, Th. 'The time-scheme of Tristram Shandy and a source', *Laurence Sterne*, ed. G. Rohmann, Darmstadt 1980.
Ben-Prat, Z. 'The poetics of literary allusion', *PTL: A Journal for Descriptive Poetics and Theory of Literature* 1 (1976) 105–28.
Berger, D.A. 'Das gezielte Mißverständnis: Kommunikationsprobleme in Laurence Sterne's *Tristram Shandy*', *Poetica* V (1972) 329–47.
Blumenberg, H. 'Wirklichkeitsbegriff und Möglichkeit des Romans', *Nachahmung und Illusion* (Poetik und Hermeneutik I), ed. H.R. Jauss, 2nd edn, Munich 1969.
Booth, W.C. 'The self-conscious narrator in comic fiction before *Tristram Shandy*', *PMLA* 67 (1952) 163–85.
Boswell, J. *The Life of Samuel Johnson* I, London and New York 1976.
Brady, F. 'Tristram Shandy: sexuality, morality, and sensibility', *Eighteenth-Century Studies* 4 (1970) 41–56.
Brissenden, R.F. *Virtue in Distress: Studies in the Novel of Sentiment from Richardson to Sade*, London 1974.
Brown, H.A. 'Tristram to the Hebrews: some notes on the institution of a canonic text', *Modern Language Notes* 99 (1984) 727–47.
Brückner, P. 'Sigmund Freuds Privatlektüre', *Psyche* 15 (1962).
Burckhardt, S. '*Tristram Shandy*'s law of gravity', *English Literary History* 28 (1961) 70–88.

Burke, E. *Dodsley's Annual Register* 3 (1760).

Burton, R. *The Anatomy of Melancholy*, ed. H. Jackson, New York 1977.

Butor, M. *Inventory Essays*, ed. R. Howard, New York 1968.

Byrd, M. *Tristram Shandy*, London 1985.

Caillois, R. *Man, Play, and Games*, transl. M. Barash, Glencoe 1961.

Carey, M. *Miscellaneous Essays*, 1830.

Cash, A. 'The Lockean psychology of *Tristram Shandy*', *English Literary History* 28 (1955) 125–35.

'The sermon in *Tristram Shandy*', *A Journal of English Literary History* 31 (1961) 395–417.

Coleridge, S.T. *The Literary Remains*, London and New York 1967.

Congreve, W. *The Complete Works* I, ed. M. Summers, London 1923.

Conrad, P. *Shandyism. The Character of Romantic Irony*, Oxford 1978.

Cook, A. 'Reflexive attitudes: Sterne, Gogol, Gide', *Criticism* II (Spring 1960) 164–74.

Cross, W. 'Laurence Sterne in the 20th century', *Yale Review N.S.* 15 (1925–6).

The Life and Times of Laurence Sterne, 3rd edn, New York 1967.

Cumberland, R. *Memoirs Written by Himself*, 1806.

Davis, R.G. 'Sterne and the delineation of the modern novel', *The Winged Skull. Papers from the Laurence Sterne Bicentenary Conference*, eds. A.H. Cash and J.M. Stedmond, London 1971.

DePorte, M.V. 'Digressions and madness in *A Tale of A Tub* and *Tristram Shandy*', *Huntington Library Quarterly* 34 (1970) 43–57.

Nightmares and Hobbyhorses: Swift, Sterne, and Augustan Ideas of Madness, San Marino, Ca. 1974.

Dyson, A.E. 'Sterne. The novelist as a jester', *Critical Quarterly* 4 (1962) 309–20.

Farrell, W.J. 'Nature versus art as a comic pattern in *Tristram Shandy*', *English Literary History* 30/1 (1963) 16–32.

Ferriar, J. *Illustrations of Sterne*, 2nd edn, London 1812, repr. London 1974.

Fielding, H. *The History of Tom Jones* I, ed. G. Saintsbury, Everyman's Library, London 1962.

The Covent-Garden Journal I, March 7, 1752, ed. G.E. Jensen, New York 1964.

Fink, E. *Spiel als Weltsymbol*, Stuttgart 1960.

Fluchère, H. *Laurence Sterne: From Tristram to Yorick*, transl. B. Bray, London 1965.

Forster, E.M. *Aspects of the Novel*, London 1958.

Foucault, M. *The Order of Things*, English translation, New York 1970.

Fredman, A. *Diderot and Sterne*, New York 1955.

Freedman, W.   '*Tristram Shandy*: the art of literary counterpoint', *Modern Language Quarterly* 32 (1971) 268–80.
   Laurence Sterne and the Origins of the Musical Novel, Athens 1978.
Freud, S.   *The Standard Edition of the Complete Psychological Works of Sigmund Freud* XII, transl. under the general editorship of J. Strachey in collaboration with Anna Freud et al., London 1961.
Gadamer, H.-G.   *Wahrheit und Methode*, Tübingen 1960.
Garvey, J.W.   'Laurence Sterne's wordplay', *Derbyshire Archaeological Journal* 36 (1975) 273 A.
Gombrich, G.H.   *Meditations on a Hobby Horse and other Essays on the Theory of Art*, London 1965.
Goodman, N.   *Ways of Worldmaking*, Hassocks 1978.
Graves, L.V.   'Locke's changeling and the Shandy bull', *Philological Quarterly* 60 (1981) 257–64.
Griffin, R.J.   '*Tristram Shandy* and language', *College English* 23 (Nov. 1961) 108–12.
Gysin, F.   *Model as Motif in Tristram Shandy*, Berne 1983.
Hall, J.J.   'The Hobby-horsical world of *Tristram Shandy*', *Modern Language Quarterly* 24 (1963) 131–43.
Hartley, L.   *Laurence Sterne. A Biographical Essay*, Chapel Hill 1943.
Holland, N.   'The laughter of Laurence Sterne', *Hudson Review* 9 (1956) 422–30.
Holtz, W.V.   *Image and Immortality: A Study of Tristram Shandy*, Providence 1970.
Hörhammer, D.   *Die Formation des literarischen Humors*, Munich 1984.
Howes, A.B. (ed.)   *Sterne. The Critical Heritage*, London 1974.
   Yorick and the Critics. Sterne's Reputation in England, Yale University Press 1958.
Hume, D.   *The Letters of David Hume* II, ed. J.Y.T. Grieg, Oxford 1932.
   A Treatise of Human Nature, ed. L.A. Selby-Bigge, Oxford 1968.
Hunter, J.P.   'Response as Reformation: *Tristram Shandy* and the art of interruption', *Laurence Sterne*, ed. G. Rohmann, Darmstadt 1980.
Hunting, R.   'Laurence Sterne and Virginia Woolf', *Etudes Anglaises* 32 (1979) 283–93.
Jackson, H.J.   'Sterne, Burton, and Ferriar: allusions to the Anatomy of Melancholy in volumes five to nine of *Tristram Shandy*', *Philological Quarterly* 54 (1975) 457–70.
Jean Paul   *Horn of Oberon. Jean Paul Richter's School for Aesthetics*, transl. M.R. Hale, Detroit 1973.
Jefferson, D.W.   '*Tristram Shandy* and the tradition of learned wit', *Essays in Criticism* 1 (1951) 225–48.
Johnson, S.   *A Dictionary of English Language* II, 1755, repr. Hildesheim 1968.

Jolas, E. 'My friend James Joyce', *James Joyce: Two Decades of Criticism*, ed. S. Givens, New York 1959.

Kant, I. *Critique of Pure Reason*, transl. J.M.D. Meiklejohn, Everyman's Library, London 1950.

Koselleck, R. *Kritik und Krise*, Freiburg 1959.

Krieger, M. *Poetic Presence and Illusion*, Baltimore and London 1979.

Laird, J. 'Shandean philosophy', *Philosophical Incursions into English Literature*, Cambridge 1946, 74–91.

Lamb, J. 'Sterne's system of imitation', *Modern Language Review* 76 (1981) 794–810.

  'The comic sublime and Sterne's fiction', *English Literary History* 48 (1981) 110–43.

Lange, V. 'Erzählformen im Roman des achtzehnten Jahrhunderts', *Henry Fielding und der englische Roman des 18. Jahrhunderts*, ed. W. Iser, Darmstadt 1972.

Lanham, R.A. *'Tristram Shandy': The Games of Pleasure*, Berkeley, Los Angeles and London 1973.

Lehman, B.H. 'Of time, personality and the author', *Laurence Sterne: A Collection of Critical Essays*, ed. J. Traugott, Englewood Cliffs 1968.

Lotman, J. *Die Struktur literarischer Texte*, Munich 1972.

Loveridge, M. *Laurence Sterne and the Argument about Design*. London 1982.

Lugowski, C. *Die Form der Individualität im Roman*, Berlin 1932.

Lukács, G. *Die Theorie des Romans*, Neuwied 1963.

Maack, R. *Laurence Sterne im Lichte seiner Zeit*, Hamburg 1936.

McKillop, A.D. 'The reinterpretation of Laurence Sterne', *Second International Conference of University Professors of English*, Paris (August 1953) 38–40.

McMaster, J. 'From experience to expression. Thematic character contrasts in *Tristram Shandy*', *Modern Language Quarterly* 32 (1971) 42–57.

Maskell, D. 'Locke and Sterne, or, can philosophy influence literature?', *Essays in Criticism* 23 (1973) 22–39.

Meyer, H. *The Poetics of Quotation in the European Novel*, Princeton 1968.

Miller, N. 'Die Rollen des Erzählers. Zum Problem des Romananfangs im 18. Jahrhundert', *Romananfänge. Versuch zu einer Poetik des Romans*, ed. N. Miller, Berlin 1965.

Moglen, H. *The Philosophical Irony of Laurence Sterne*, Gainesville 1975.

Montadou, A. *La Réception de Laurence Sterne en Allemagne*, Clermont-Ferrand 1985.

Nanner, T. *Identität und Idee. Laurence Sterne's Tristram Shandy*, Heidelberg 1975.

  'Laurence Sterne auf den zweiten Blick', *Anglia* 96 (1978) 65–88.

Nänny, M. 'Similarity and contiguity in *Tristram Shandy*', *English Studies* 60 (1979) 422–35.

New, M. *Laurence Sterne as Satirist: A Reading of Tristram Shandy*, Gainesville 1975.

Nietzsche, F. *Human, All Too Human. A Book for Free Spirits*, transl. R.J. Hollingdale, Cambridge 1986.

Paulson, R. 'Sterne. The subversion' and 'Yorick from self-revelation to self-analysis', *Satire and the Novel in Eighteenth-Century England*. New Haven and London 1967, 248–65.

Petrie, G. 'Rhetoric as fictional technique in *Tristram Shandy*', *Philological Quarterly* 48 (1969) 479–94.

Pinger, W.R.R. *Laurence Sterne and Goethe*, Pittsburgh 1969.

Piper, W.B. *Laurence Sterne*, New York 1965.

Plessner, H. *Die Stufen des Organischen und der Mensch*, 2nd edn, Berlin 1965.

Posner, R. 'Semiotic paradoxes in language use with particular reference to *Tristram Shandy*', *The Eighteenth Century: Theory and Interpretation* 20 (1979) 148–63.

Preisendanz, W. 'Humor als Rolle', *Identität* (Poetik und Hermeneutik VIII), eds. O. Marquard and K. Stierle, Munich 1979.

Preston, J. *The Created Self. The Reader's Role in Eighteenth-Century Fiction*, London 1970.

Putney, R. 'Laurence Sterne, apostle of laughter', *The Age of Johnson. Essays presented to Chauncey Brewster Tinker*, ed. F.W. Hillers, New Haven 1949, 159–70.

Reid, B. 'The sad hilarity of Sterne', *Virginia Quarterly Review* 32 (1956) 107–30.

Richardson, S. *Selected Letters of Samuel Richardson*, ed. J. Caroll, London 1964.

Rohmann, G. 'Die zeitgenössische Rezeption (1760–1813)', *Laurence Sterne*, ed. G. Rohmann, Darmstadt 1980.

Rohrberger, M. and Woods, S. 'Alchemy of the word: surrealism in *Tristram Shandy*', *Interpretations* 11 (1979) 24–34.

Rosenblum, M. 'Shandean geometry and contingency', *Novel* 10 (1977) 237–47.

Rousseau, G.S. 'Science', *The Eighteenth Century*, ed. P. Rogers, London 1978.

Rubin, L.D. Jr. 'Joyce and Sterne: a study in affinity', *The Hopkins Review* 3 (1950) 14–22.

Russell, H.K. '*Tristram Shandy* and the technique of the novel', *Studies in Philology* 42 (1945) 581–93.

Schopenhauer, A. *Parerga and Paralipomena. Short Philosophical Essays* II, transl. E.F.J. Payne, Oxford 1974.

Schwab, G. *Entgrenzungen und Entgrenzungsmythen. Zur Subjektivität im modernen Roman*, Stuttgart 1987.

Scott, Sir Walter *The Miscellaneous Prose Works* I, Edinburgh 1854.

Shaw, M.R.B. *Laurence Sterne, the Making of a Humourist*, London 1957.

Shklovsky, V. 'A parodying novel: Sterne's *Tristram Shandy*, *Laurence Sterne: A Collection of Critical Essays*, ed. J. Traugott, Englewood Cliffs 1968.

Simon, E. 'Fatalism, the hobby-horse and the esthetics of the novel', *Diderot Studies* 16 (1973) 253–74.

Smith, A. *The Theory of Moral Sentiments* (The Glasgow edition of the Works and Correspondence I), eds. D.D. Raphael and A.L. Macfie, Oxford 1976.

Stedmond, J.M. *The Comic Art of Laurence Sterne: Convention and Innovation in 'Tristram Shandy' and 'A Sentimental Journey'*, Toronto 1967.

Sterne, L. *Letters of Laurence Sterne*, ed. L.P. Curtis, Oxford 1935.

Swearingen, J.E. *Reflexivity in Tristram Shandy*, New Haven and London 1977.

Tave, S.M. *The Amiable Humorist*, Chicago 1967.

Thackeray, W.M. *The Lectures on the English Humourists* (*The Works* XI, Centenary Biographical Edition), ed. Lady Ritchie, London 1911.

Traugott, J. *Tristram Shandy's World*, Berkeley and Los Angeles 1954.

Walpole, H. *Horace Walpole's Correspondence with Sir David Dalrymple*, eds. W.S. Lewis and C.H. Bennett and A.G. Hoover, New York 1951.

Warning, R. *Illusion und Wirklichkeit in Tristram Shandy und Jacques le Fataliste*, Munich 1965.

Warren, L. 'The constant speaker: aspects of conversation in *Tristram Shandy*', *University of Toronto Quarterly* 46 (1976) 51–67.

Watt, I. 'The comic syntax of *Tristram Shandy*', *Studies in Criticism and Aesthetics 1660–1800: Essays in Honor of Samuel Holt Monk*, eds. H. Anderson and J.S. Shea, Minneapolis 1967.

Wieland, C.M. *Ausgewählte Briefe von C.M. Wieland, an verschiedene Freunde in den Jahren 1751–1810 geschrieben und nach der Zeitfolge geordnet* II, Zurich 1815.

Woolf, V. *The Common Reader. Second Series*, 7th edn, London 1959. *A Writer's Diary. Being Extracts from the Diary of Virginia Woolf*, ed. L. Woolf, London 1953.

Wright, A. 'The artifice of failure in *Tristram Shandy*', *Novel* 2 (1969) 212–20.

Yoseloff, Th. *A Fellow of Infinite Jest*, Englewood Cliffs 1945.